SAVAGE OF THE SEA

BOOK ONE: PIRATES OF BRITANNIA - LORDS OF THE SEA

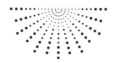

ELIZA KNIGHT

KNIGHT
MEDIA

~

Lords of the sea. A daring brotherhood, where honor among thieves reigns supreme, and crushing their enemies is a thrilling pastime. These are the pirates of Britannia.

When Highland pirate prince Shaw "Savage" MacDougall is invited to a deadly feast, he doesn't know that saving a wee lass could forever change his future.

Widowed at a young age, Lady Jane Lindsey seeks refuge from her departed husband's vengeful enemies. For five years, she's held a secret that could cost her everything, including her life. When her safety is compromised, she reaches out to the only man who's protected her in the past and offers him a bounty he cannot refuse.

Shaw's life is perfect. Whisky, women and mayhem. He wants for nothing—until Lady Jane presents a treasure he'd never considered possessing. He'll have to risk his lethal reputation in order to save a lass he barely knows, *again*. And she'll have to trust a pirate to see their arrangement through to the end. But what happens when perilous battles turn to sinful kisses? Who will save them from each other?

Dear Reader,

Welcome to a fun new series! I'm so excited for you all to join Kathryn Le Veque and myself on our new adventure. Highlanders and knights upon the sea! An epic saga that is sure to be thrilling, daring and sexy!

The legend of King Arthur MacAlpin is purely fictional and a great jumping off point for this new series. You'll find that my hero is a MacDougall, and a descendent of my MacDougall heroes, though his father, who I've made into a less than stellar specimen, is certainly not one of my previous heroes!

I based the opening chapter of this story on the infamous Black Dinner that took place in 1440. While there is no mention of whether the fifteen/sixteen year old William, Earl of Douglas brought his young countess bride with him to the dinner, for the purposes of this story, I have placed her there, and given her a home and a happily-ever-after in my story. The Black Knight of Lorne is a real character, and he was married to Queen Joan, and the events recalling her death are all true. The Black Knight was even kidnapped by pirates, which was perfect fodder for my story, and which I took creative license in adding to the story.

While the Isle of Scarba is a real place, my fictional Castle Dheomhan was created as in my mind for Savage's stronghold.

I do hope you enjoyed the first book in this new series!

Happy Reading,

Eliza

LEGEND OF THE PIRATES OF BRITANNIA

In the year of our Lord 854, a wee lad by the name of Arthur MacAlpin set out on an adventure that would turn the tides of his fortune, for what could be more exciting than being feared and showered with gold?

Arthur wanted to be king. A sovereign as great as King Arthur, who came hundreds of years before him. The legendary knight who was able to pull a magical sword from stone, met ladies in lakes and vanquished evil with a vast following who worshipped him. But while *that* King Arthur brought to mind dreamlike images of a roundtable surrounded by chivalrous knights and the ladies they romanced, MacAlpin wanted to summon night terrors from every babe, woman and man.

Aye, MacAlpin, king of the pirates of Britannia would be a name most feared. A name that crossed children's lips when the candles were blown out at night. When a shadow passed over a wall, was it the pirate king? When a ship sailed into port in the dark hours of night, was it him?

As the fourth son of the conquering Pictish King Cináed, Arthur wanted to prove himself to his father. He wanted to make his father proud, and show him that he, too, could be a conqueror. King Cináed was praised widely for having run off the Vikings, for saving his people, for amassing a vast and strong army. No one would dare encroach on his conquered lands when they would have to face the end of his blade.

Arthur wanted that, too. He wanted to be feared. Awed. To hold his sword up and have devils come flying from the tip.

So, it was on a fateful summer night in 854, that at the age of ten and nine, Arthur amassed a crew of young and roguish Picts and stealthily commandeered one of his father's ships. They blackened the sails to hide them from those on watch and began an adventure that would last a lifetime and beyond.

The lads trolled the seas, boarding ships and sacking small coastal villages. In fact, they even sailed so far north as to raid a Viking village in the name of his father. By the time they returned to Oban, and the seat of King Cináed, all of Scotland was raging about Arthur's atrocities. Confused, he tried to explain, but his father would not listen and would not allow him back into the castle.

King Cináed banished his youngest son from the land, condemned his acts as evil and told him he never wanted to see him again.

Enraged and experiencing an underlying layer of mortification, Arthur took to the seas, gathering men as he went, and building a family he could trust would not shun him. They ravaged the sea as well as the land—using his clan's name as a lasting insult to his father for turning him out.

The legendary Pirate King was rumored to be merciless, the type of vengeful pirate who would drown a babe in his mother's own milk if she didn't give him the pearls at her neck. But with most rumors, they were mostly steeped in falsehoods meant to intimidate. In fact, there may have been a wee boy or two he saved from an untimely fate. Whenever they came across a lad or lass in need, as Arthur himself had once been, they took them into the fold.

One ship became two. And then three, four, five, until a score of ships with blackened sails roamed the seas.

These were *his* warriors. A legion of men who adored him, respected him, followed him, and together they wreaked havoc on the blood ties that had sent him away. And generations upon generations, country upon country, they would spread far and wide until people feared them from horizon to horizon. Every pirate king to follow would be named MacAlpin, so his father's banishment would never be forgotten.

Forever lords of the Sea. A daring brotherhood, where honor among thieves reigns supreme, and crushing their enemies is a thrilling pastime.

These are the pirates of Britannia, and here are their stories...

CHAPTER ONE

Edinburgh Castle, Scotland
November 1440

Shaw MacDougall stood in the great hall of Edinburgh Castle with dread in the pit of his stomach. He was amongst dozens of other armored knights—though he was no knight. Nay, he was a blackmailed pirate under the guise of a mercenary for the day. And though he'd not known the job he was hired to do until he arrived at the castle, and still didn't really. He'd been told to wait until given an order, and ever since, the leather-studded armor weighed heavily on him, and sweat dripped in a steady line down his spine.

The wee King of Scotland, just ten summers, sat at the dais entertaining his guests, who were but children themselves. William Douglas, Earl of Douglas, was only sixteen, and his brother was only a year or two older than the king himself. Beside the lads was a beautiful young lass, with long golden locks that caught the light of the torches. The lass was perhaps no more than sixteen herself, though she already had a woman's body—a body he should most certainly *not* be looking at. And though he was only a handful of years over twenty, and might be convinced she was of age, he was positive she was far too young for him. Wide blue eyes flashed from her face and held the gaze of everyone in the room just long enough that they were left squirming. And her mouth... God, she had a mouth made to—

Ballocks! It was wrong to look at her in any way that might be construed as...desire.

There was an air of innocence about her that clashed with the cynical look she sometimes cast the earl, whom Shaw had guessed might be her husband. It wasn't hard to spot a woman unhappily married. Hell, it was a skill he'd honed while in port, as he loved to dally with disenchanted wives and leave them quite satisfied.

Unfortunately for him, he was not interested in wee virginal lasses. And so, would not be leaving *that* lass satisfied. Decidedly, he kept his gaze averted from her and eyed the men about the room.

Torches on the perimeter walls lit the great hall, but only dimly. None of the candelabras were burning, leaving many parts of the room cast in shadow—the corners in particular. And for Shaw, this was quite disturbing.

He was no stranger to battle—and not just any type of battle—he was intimately acquainted with guerilla warfare, the *pirate* way. But why the hell would he, the prince of pirates, be hired by a noble lord intimately acquainted with the king?

Shaw glanced sideways at the man who'd hired him. Sir Andrew Livingstone. Shaw's payment wasn't in coin, nay, he'd taken this mission in exchange for several members of his crew being released from the dungeons without a trial. Had he not, they'd likely have hung. Shaw had been more than happy to strike a bargain with Livingstone in exchange for his men's lives.

Now, he dreaded the thought of what that job might be.

This would be the last time he let his men convince him mooring in Blackness Bay for a night of debauchery was a good idea. It was there that two of his crew had decided to act like drunken fools, and it was also there, that half a dozen other pirates jumped in to save them. They'd all been arrested and brought before Livingstone, who'd tossed them in a cell.

And now, here he was, feeling out of place in the presence of the king and the two men, Livingstone and the Lord Chancellor, who had arranged for this oddly dark feast. They kept giving each other strange looks, as though speaking through gestures. Shaw shifted, cracking his neck, and glanced back at the dais table lined with youthful nobles.

Seated beside the young earl, the lass glanced furtively around the room, her eyes jumpy as a rabbit as though she sensed something. She sipped her cup daintily and picked at the food on her plate, peeking nervously about the room. Every once in a while, she'd give her head a little shake as if trying to convince herself that whatever it was she sensed was all in her head.

The air in the room shifted, growing tenser. There was a subtle nod from the Lord Chancellor to a man near the back of the room, who then disappeared. At the same time, a knight approached the lass with a message. She wrinkled her nose, glancing back toward the young lad to her left and shaking her head, dismissing the knight. But a second later, she was escorted, rather unwillingly, from the room.

Shaw tensed at the way the knight gripped her arm and that her idiotic boy husband didn't seem to care at all. What was the meaning of all this?

Perhaps the reason presented itself a moment later. A

man dressed in black from head to toe, including a hood covering his face, entered from the rear of the great hall carrying a blackened boar's head on a platter. He walked slowly, and as those sitting at the table turned their gaze toward him, their eyes widened. In what though? Shock? Curiosity? Or was it fear?

Did Livingstone plan to kill the king?

If so, why did none of the guards pull out their swords to stop this messenger of death?

Shaw was finding it difficult to stand by and let this happen.

But the man in black did not stop in front of the king. Instead, he stopped in front of the young earl and his wee brother, placing the boar's head between them. Shaw knew what it meant before either of the victims it was served to did.

"Nay," he growled under his breath.

The two lads looked at the blackened head with disgust, and then the earl seemed to recognize the menacing gesture. Glowering at the servant, he said, "Get that bloody thing out of my sight."

Shaw was taken aback that the young man spoke with such authority, though he supposed at sixteen, he himself had already captained one of MacAlpin's ships and posed that same authority.

At this, Livingstone and Crichton stood and took their places before the earl and his brother.

"William Douglas, sixth Earl of Douglas, and Sir David Douglas, ye're hereby charged with treason against His Majesty King James II."

The young king worked hard to hide his surprise, sitting up a little taller. "What? Nay!"

The earl glanced at the king with a sneer one gives a child they think deserves punishment. "What charges could ye have against us?" Douglas shouted. "We've done nothing wrong. We are loyal to our king."

"Ye stand before your accusers and deny the charges?" Livingstone said, eyebrow arched, his tone brooking no argument.

"*What* charges?" Douglas's face had turned red with rage, and he stood, hands fisted at his sides.

Livingstone slammed his hands down on the table in front of Douglas. "Guilty. Ye're guilty."

William Douglas jerked to a stand, shoving his brother behind him, and pulled his sword from its scabbard. "Lies!" He lunged forward and would have been able to do damage to his accusers if not for the seasoned warriors who over-powered him from behind.

"Stop," King James shouted, his small voice drowned out by the screams of the Douglas lads and the shouts of the warriors.

Quickly overpowered, the noble lads were dragged kicking and screaming from the great hall, all while King James shouted for the spectacle to cease.

Shaw was about to follow the crowd outside when Livingstone gripped his arm.

"Take care of Lady Douglas."

Lady Douglas. The sixteen-year-old countess.

"Take care?" Shaw needed to hear it explicitly.

"Aye. Execute her. I dinna care how. Just see it done." The man shrugged. "We were going to let her live, but I've changed my mind. Might as well get her out of the way, too."

Livingstone wanted Shaw to kill her? As though it was acceptable for a lord to execute lads on trumped up charges of treason, but the murder of a lass, that was a pirate's duty.

Shaw ground his teeth and nodded. Killing innocent lassies wasn't part of his code. He'd never done so before and didn't want to start now. Blast it all! Six pirates for one wee lass. One beautiful, enchanting lass who'd never done him harm. Hell, he didn't even know her. Slipping unnoticed past the bloodthirsty crowd wasn't hard given they were too intent on the insanity unfolding around them. He made his way toward the arch where he'd seen the lass dragged too not a quarter hour before.

The arch led to a dimly lit rounded staircase and the only way to go was up. Pulling his *sgian-dubh* from his boot, Shaw hurried up the stairs, his soft boots barely a whisper on every stone step. At the first round, he encountered a closed door. An ear pressed against the wood proved no one inside. He went up three more stairs to another quiet room. He continued to climb, listening at every door until he reached the very top. The door was closed, and it was quiet, but the air was charged making the hair on the back of his neck prickle.

Taking no more time, Shaw shouldered the door open to find the knight who'd escorted the lass from the great hall lying on top of her on the floor. They struggled. Her legs were parted, skirts up around her hips, tears of rage on her reddened face. The bastard had a hand over her mouth and sneered up at Shaw upon his entry.

Fury boiled inside him. Shaw slammed the door shut so hard it rattled the rafters.

"Get up," Shaw demanded, rage pummeling through him at having caught the man as he tried to rape the lass.

Tears streamed from her eyes, which blazed blue as she stared at him. Her face was pale, and her limbs were trembling. Still, there was defiance in the set of her jaw. Something inside his chest clenched. He wanted to rip the whoreson limb from limb. And he knew for a fact he wasn't going to kill Lady Douglas.

"I said get up." Shaw advanced a step or two, averting his

eyes for a moment as the knight removed himself from her person, letting her adjust her skirts down her legs.

Shaw waved his hand at her, indicating she should run from the room, but rather than escape, she went to the corner of the chamber and cowered.

Saints, but his heart went out to her.

Shaw was a pirate, had witnessed a number of savage acts, and the one thing he could never abide by was the rape of a woman.

The knight didn't speak, instead he charged toward Shaw with murder in his eyes.

But that didn't matter. Shaw had dealt with a number of men like him who were used to preying on women. He would be easy, and he would bear the entire brutal brunt of Shaw's ire.

Shaw didn't move, simply waiting the breath it took for the knight to be on him. He leapt to the left, out of the path of the knight's blade, and sank his own blade in quick succession into the man's gut, then heart, then neck. Three rapid jabs.

The knight fell to the ground, blood pouring from his wounds, his eyes and mouth wide in surprise. Too easy.

"Please," the lass whimpered from the corner. The defiance that had shown on her face before disappeared, and now she only looked frightened. "Please, dinna hurt me."

"I would never. Ye have my word." Shaw tried to make his words soothing, but they came out so gruff, he was certain they were exactly the opposite.

He wiped the blood from his blade onto the knight's hose and then stuck the *sgian-dubh* back into his boot. He approached the lass, hands outstretched, as he might a wild filly. "We must go, lass."

"Please, go." She wiped at the blood on her lips. "Leave me here."

"Lady Jane, is that right?" he asked, ignoring her plea for him to leave her.

She nodded.

"I need to get ye out of here. I was..." Should he tell her? "I was sent by Livingstone to...take your life. But I willna. I swear it. Come now, we must escape."

"What?" Her tears ceased in her surprise.

"Ye canna be seen. The lads, your husband..." Shaw ran a hand through his hair. "Livingstone willna let them leave alive. He doesna want *ye* to leave alive."

That defiance returned to her striking blue eyes as she stared him down. "I dinna believe ye."

"Trust me."

She shook her head and slid slowly up the wall to stand, her hands braced on the stone behind her. "Where is my husband?"

Shaw grimaced. "He's gone, lass. Come now, or ye'll be gone soon, too." He'd not been hired for this task, to take a shaking lass out of castle and hide her away. But the alternative was much worse. And he'd not be committing the murder of an innocent today.

Indeed, he risked his entire reputation by being here and doing anything at all, but he was pretty certain the two lads she'd arrived with were dead already, and along with them the rest of their party. Livingstone and Crichton weren't about to let the lass live to tell the tale or rally the rest of the Douglas clan to come after them. That line was healthy, long and powerful.

"I dinna understand," she mumbled. "Who are ye?"

"I am Shaw MacDougall."

She searched his eyes, seeking understanding and not finding it. "I dinna know ye."

"All ye need to know is I am here to get ye to safety. Come now. They'll be looking for ye soon." And him. This was a

8

direct breach of their contract, and Livingstone would not stop until he had Shaw's head on a spike.

But Shaw didn't care. He hated the bastard and had been looking for retribution. Let that be a lesson to Livingstone for attempting to blackmail a pirate. His men would be proud to know he'd not succumbed to the blackguard's demands. As he stood there, they were already being broken out of the jail at Blackness Bay.

Stopping a few feet in front of the lass, he held out his hand and gestured for her to take it. She shook her head.

"Lady Jane, I canna begin to understand what ye're feeling right now, but I also canna stress enough the urgency of the situation. I've a horse, and my ship is not far from here. Come now, else surrender your fate to that of your husband."

"William."

"He is dead, lass. Or soon to be."

"Nay..." Her chin wobbled, and she looked ready to collapse.

"Aye. There is no time to argue. Come. I will carry ye if ye need me to."

Perhaps it would be better if he simply lifted her up and tossed her over his shoulder. Shaw made a move to reach for her when she shook her head and straightened her shoulders.

"Will ye take me to Iona, Sir MacDougall?"

"Aye. Will Livingstone know to look for ye there?"

She shook her head. "My aunt is a nun there. Livingstone may put it together at some point, but I will be safe there for now."

"Aye."

"Oh..." She started to tremble uncontrollably. "Oh my... I... I'm going to..." And then she fell into his arms, unconscious.

Shaw let out a sigh and tossed her over his shoulder as

he'd thought to do just a few moments before. Hopefully, she'd not wake until they were on his ship and had already set sail. He sneaked back down the stairs, and rather than go out the front where he could hear screams of pain and shouts filled with the thirst for blood, he snuck her out the postern gate at the back of the castle. He half ran, half slid down the steep slope, thanking the heavens every second when the lass did not waken.

Though he'd arrived at the castle on a horse, he'd had one of his men ride with another and instructed him to wait at the bottom of the castle hill in case he needed to make an escape. Some might say he had a sixth sense about such things, but he preferred to say that he simply had a pirate's sense of preservation.

Livingstone was a blackguard who'd made a deal with a pirate to commit murder. A powerful lord only made dealings with a pirate when he needed muscle at his back. And when he chose to keep his own hands clean. But that didn't mean Livingstone wouldn't hesitate killing Shaw.

Well, Livingstone was a fool. And Shaw was not. There was his horse waiting for him at the bottom of the hill just as he'd asked.

"Just as ye said, Cap'n," Jack, his quartermaster—called so for being a Jack-of-all-trades—said with a wide, toothy grin. "What's that?"

Shaw raised a brow, glancing at the rounded feminine arse beside his face. "A lass. Let's go."

"Oh, taken to kidnapping now, aye?"

"Not exactly." Shaw tossed the lass up onto the horse and climbed up behind her. "Come on, Jack. Back to the ship."

They took off at a canter, loping through the dirt-packed roads of Edinburgh toward the Water of Leith that led out to the Firth of Forth and the sea beyond. But then on second thought, he veered his horse to the right. When they rowed their skiff up the Leith to get to the castle, they'd had more time. Now, time was of the essence, and riding their horses straight to the docks at the Forth where his ship awaited would be quicker. No doubt, as soon as Livingstone noticed Shaw was gone—as well as the girl—he'd send a horde of men after him. Shaw could probably convince a few of them to join his crew, but he didn't have time for that.

A quarter of an hour later, their horses covered in a sheen of sweat, Shaw shouted for his men to lower the gangplank, and he rode the horse right up onto the main deck of the *Savage of the Sea*, his pride and joy, the ship he'd captained since he was not much older than the lass he carried.

"Avast ye, maties! All hands hoy! Weigh anchor and hoist the mizzen. Ignore the wench and get us the hell out of here. To Iona we sail!" With his instructions given, Shaw carried the still unconscious young woman up the few stairs to his own quarters, pushing open the door and slamming it shut behind him.

There, he paused. If he set her on the bed, what would she think when she woke? What would he think if he saw her there? She was much too young for him, aye. But whenever he brought a wench to his quarters and laid her on the bed, it was not for any bit of *saving*, unless it was release from the tension pleasure built.

And yet, the floor did not seem like a good spot, either.

He settled for the long wooden bench at the base of his bed.

As soon as he laid her there, her eyes popped open, and she leapt to her feet. "What are ye doing? Where have ye taken me?" She looked about her wildly, reaching for nothing and everything at once. Blond locks flying wildly.

"Calm yourself, lass." Shaw raised a sardonic brow. "We sail for Iona as ye requested. And from there, we shall part ways."

She eyed him suspiciously. "And nothing more?"

He crossed his arms over his chest and studied her. As the seconds ticked past, her shoulders seemed to sag a little more, and that crazed look evaporated from her eyes. "Nothing save the satisfaction that I have taken ye from a man who would have done ye harm."

"Livingstone?"

"Aye."

Her lower lip trembled. "Aye. He will want to kill all who bear the Douglas name."

Shaw's eyes lowered to her flat belly. "Might there be another?" he asked.

She shook her head violently. "Ye saved me just before that awful man could…"

"Ye misunderstand me, my lady. I meant your husband's…" Ballocks, why did he find it hard to say the word *seed* to the lass? He was a bloody pirate and far more vulgar words, to any number of wenches, had come from his mouth.

She lifted her chin, jutting it forward obstinately. "There is nothing."

Shaw chose to take her word for it rather than discuss the intimate relationship she might have had with her boy husband and when the last time her courses had come. "Then ye need only worry about your own neck, and no one else's."

He expected her to fall into a puddle of tears, but she didn't.

The lass simply nodded and then said, "I owe ye a debt, Sir MacDougall."

"Call me Savage, lass. And rest assured, I will collect."

CHAPTER TWO

November 1441

*D*ear Savage of the Sea,
        I deplore writing that out, but as it is the name you bid me address you, who am I to give you another? I write on this, the one year anniversary of having arrived at Iona via your impressive ship. And given I am still safely ensconced, I must thank you for seeing me brought here, as well as for keeping the secret of my whereabouts. I am reminded on this one-year mark, that I still owe you a debt, and I did not want you to think I had forgotten.

The nuns at Iona treat me well, though they are irritated I have not yet chosen to take vows. As such, I'm certain they give me the worst of all chores. But I do them with a glad heart because I am alive, and I know more so than any other woman here that life is precious. Except perhaps that of Sister Maria. I've yet to learn her story. She thinks me too young. I am almost seventeen though, and I've been married before, which I'm certain she has not. Does that not make me more of a grown up?

Well, I am rambling, and I'm certain that a man of your trade has no use for ramblings.

I bid you adieu.

Yours in debt,

Lady Marina (I have often caught myself saying my true name, so much so, that I'm certain at least three of the sisters at Iona believe my name to be Jamarina.)

MARCH 1442

Dear Jamarina,

I quite like your new moniker. I was at sea many months, traveling near India. An exotic place to be certain, though too hot for my tastes. I've only just returned and received your missive.

It is good to know you are safe, and trust that your secret is safe with me, for we are both hunted by the same rat. Alas, I am the hawk that feeds on vermin.

Perhaps your Sister Maria has a secret as profound as yours. Perhaps she only toys with you.

I have not forgotten our debt, but I have not had cause to call upon you for it.

As you say, you are only just a lass of seventeen.

Yours in service,

What name would you give me?

JUNE 1442

Dear Gentle Warrior,

Aye, I believe I quite like that.

I confess I was surprised that you returned my letter. I had not thought a man of your trade to possess such beautiful script.

Sister Maria is gone. In the middle of the night. Mother Superior will not tell us what happened, and neither will my aunt. I suppose she did have a dark secret. I pray I do not disappear.

Again, they have asked me if I would take vows to become a novice nun, but there is something holding me back. I shall think on it a little longer.

Yours in debt,

Jamarina

Dearest Gentle Warrior,

I hope you are well and that I did not offend you with my last letter. If it pleases, I will not write again. But I must say thank you once more, for it has now been two years since I arrived safely at Iona.

I confess, I long to leave. I do not think a life of servitude is for me. I am a child of the Lord, to be certain, but I find myself heavy with ~~thoughts that lead me to confession~~ idle thoughts.

Yours in debt,

Jamarina

April 1443

Dearest Gentle Warrior,

I confess I am much worried over you. It has been over a year since I've heard from you.

What it must be like to sail the sea. Free from walls. Free from judgment. Free. I am still grateful for what you did for me, but I feel a heavy cloud of melancholy. A sadness and loneliness, though I am surrounded by people. Perhaps, what I long for is the open sea.

Sister Maria has come back. I should think she is hiding something, for she avoids me, though not everyone else.

Yours in debt,

Lady J

December 1443

Dearest Lass,

A pirate's life is not for thee.

I bid you good-bye until we meet again. Your last letter was read by someone other than myself.

Your Gentle Warrior

PS. I wish you well on celebrating your eighteenth year. I do not know my own birthday, so I have celebrated mine with you these past few years.

~

Isle of Iona

October 1445

The nights were normally quiet at the abbey. Lady Jane Lindsay walked the open-air cloisters between compline and matins when everyone else was sleeping, because sleep rarely came to her.

It was an issue she'd dealt with ever since that horrible night five years before, this inability to rest. And the only thing that seemed to help was walking in the nighttime air, no matter the weather, with no one present so that she could clear her mind, stare at the stars and think of a world outside these confining walls.

Sometimes it worked, and sometimes it did not.

She was Lady Marina now, her birth name of Jane a secret between herself, her aunt and the Mother Superior. Well, and her gentle warrior. She'd not written him since that day he'd warned someone else was reading her letters. And ever since she'd stopped, the scornful gazes she'd been receiving from Mother Superior had subsided. Was it she who read the letters?

Marina had been on Iona since the day the pirate prince had left her at the shore just before dawn so none of the sisters at the abbey would be able to identify her rescuer. And though five years had passed in the company of the devoted women of God, Marina had yet to take formal vows herself. Though not for Mother Superior's lack of trying. She wasn't certain what held her back, only that she felt destined for something, and she'd yet to figure out what. Perhaps the overarching fear of discovery had been at the heart of that desire to keep herself free and separate from the women who had taken her in.

She'd once thought that she might like a life at sea. Those few days upon the *Savage of the Sea* had been the most peaceful of her life. No one had looked at her as though she were a pawn. No one had expected to use her, as had been her lot since the day she was born. Surprisingly, not even Shaw MacDougall, who she owed a debt.

For now, she knew that their lives could be in danger.

Even that rakishly handsome devil prince of pirates did not know the true danger she was in. The secret that would have made Livingstone want her dead. She'd kept that from Shaw. The less people who knew, the better.

Och, but she had thought of him often over the years. Her gentle warrior. The way he'd gazed at her with barely restrained longing, seeing the shame in his eyes for having done so. The way he'd gone against direct orders from Livingstone in order to save her. And who was she to him other than a lass?

The days she'd spent on his ship, he'd talked with her, played cards and knucklebones with her. She'd even taken two nights to read to him as the sun set. Their connection had been oddly easy and fluid. It had felt right. But then she'd had to leave him, and she wondered if maybe she'd only made up that connection after having an arrogant pig for a husband. Dare she call Shaw a friend?

She thought so. And given the fearsome pirate had been

willing to write a naïve lass when she sent him letters, well, that proved it, didn't it?

Jane dropped to her knees where she was in the center of the cloister and stared up at the sky. She had to leave. And yet, she could not leave without the help of the man who'd brought her here. And there was only one way to get him to return to her. To help her.

She owed *him* a debt, and she was certain a pirate would never forget his debts. Especially those owed to him. And now, she would need him to do her another favor. But only if it were worth his while. That morning she'd managed to get a missive sent off with a local fisherman. She could only pray the messenger made it back alive, and that no one intercepted her letter this time. The man had agreed to take her message, but not for free. Especially when he heard where she wanted him to go. But the sight of her ring had been enough for him to agree. She'd given him one of her precious jewels, not only as payment, but also as proof to MacDougall that it was she who'd sent for him.

"Pray, come in time," she whispered to the night air, hoping her words reached Shaw wherever he was.

But it had been five years since she'd seen him, and well over a year since she'd gotten his last letter. She'd not replied to that one, fearful of who it was that had intercepted it, and she'd been waiting every day since then for Livingstone to come crashing through the abbey doors. But her day of reckoning was coming.

The name Livingstone had not crossed her lips since the day MacDougall had saved her from the knight's vicious attack. Not even when they'd been on the ship traveling to Iona. But it had crossed Mother Superior's tongue that morning while the sisters and Jane broke their fast. His name hung in the air, causing Jane's ears to buzz. Her worst enemy was going to be making a visit to the abbey on his pilgrimage across the country. Her hands still trembled at what Mother Superior had relayed to her.

The ladies in attendance had all been pleased to hear it, for it meant more coin would be placed in the abbey's coffers. Perhaps this coming winter, they might all have newly darned hose rather than the threadbare ones they'd used the year before. But to Jane, it had meant something else entirely—certain doom.

It meant death.

For she alone knew that Livingstone was not making a pilgrimage across the country in hopes of redeeming his soul, but instead was ferreting her out. Somehow, he must have gotten word she was seeking sanctuary at an abbey. Perhaps even this abbey.

In truth, she was surprised it had taken him this long to do so. How had he found out? Who'd told him she was here? Was it whoever had read the letter? Mother Superior? Sister Maria who'd disappeared several years before? Or was he just that clever? Perhaps in the last five years, he'd left no stone unturned but those lying atop Iona.

Mayhap for a while, he'd thought her dead, or that the pirate had kidnapped her, ravaged her and done away with her by tossing her out to sea. Part of her had hoped her gentle warrior had taken flight as a hawk and sank his claws into the blackguard.

Alas, none of her dreams that would lead her to freedom had come to fruition.

But something must have made him believe she was alive, and yet, she could not guess at who or what it could be. No one here knew of her identity, save for Mother Superior and her aunt. Even in her letters, she'd not written as Jane or given any other truly identifying information.

There was always the chance that Mother might have accidentally let some piece of information slip, for though she knew that Marina was her aunt's niece and that her name was Jane, she did not know the circumstances regarding why she must be hidden.

She did not know that Livingstone had killed Jane's husband.

That he wanted to kill her.

For Jane held a dark secret. One a man would kill for.

A secret she was willing to sell to a pirate for his protection.

A secret a pirate would be willing to barter with her for.

A secret would be the undoing of an entire kingdom.

If only she could have lived out her days in peace here. But only a naïve lass would have thought such a thing. Even when she'd come here at the age of sixteen, she'd not been naïve. She'd lived the previous three years with the most arrogant of earls—her young husband. He'd treated her like rubbish. He'd disrespected her in front of his men and made sport of seeing her look dejected because it made him feel superior. Jane had been nothing more than a pawn in their marriage bargain. Betrothed at age seven and married at age thirteen, she'd spent three miserable years with William Douglas, and the only friend she'd made was his younger brother, David.

They were both dead now.

Wee David was dead by association, for possibly knowing too much. William was dead for the latter, and for his arrogance. For he'd been the one to proclaim he knew the secret. And from that moment forth, he'd had a target on his chest.

It was only by sheer instinct that Jane had thought to ask William what the big secret was, playing on his need to brag. And then he'd told her.

Now she harbored the most dangerous secret in the country.

And Livingstone knew it.

~

CASTLE DHEOMHAN, ISLE OF SCARBA

There was nothing to spoil a man's debauchery more than a messenger arriving with an urgent missive from a woman. An important woman if she knew where he resided. Besides the wenches lounging on his and his crewmen's laps, there was only one woman who had ever sent a missive to his pirate stronghold.

Gently knocking the two buxom wenches from his lap, who fell in a heap of drunken, naked laughter to the thick fur beneath his throne chair. The same throne chair that had been commissioned from steel and velvet with the Devils of the Deep skull and swords crest at its top and had parts that dated back to the original king of pirates, Arthur MacAlpin, from hundreds of years before.

Rock hard and half-drunk on whisky, Shaw settled his gaze on the messenger and willed his raging cock into submission. But that was almost impossible, given the inebriated state he was in and thinking of precious Jane. She'd be twenty-one now. Old enough that he didn't have to feel ashamed for thinking about her pert breasts and luscious mouth.

Was it she who'd sent this old man to him? Would she dare?

He'd not heard from her since his letter of warning, though he'd hoped to every day since.

But when he unrolled the parchment to behold the looping scrawl of his Lady Jane, he glanced at the messenger who stood cowering before him. This was not her usual girlish letter, but one full of desperation and a bargain.

Taking the steps down from his dais, he leaned down to look the fisherman in the eyes. "Dinna piss yourself."

"I willna, my...my... Your Highness."

21

Shaw grunted, sneering and not bothering to correct the old man. "How do I know this is not a trick?"

The fisherman stepped forward, reaching for his sporran. A bad idea in a room full of men expecting weapons to be drawn at any moment, and the old bastard was awarded with a dozen sharp blades at his throat.

The bloke raised his arms, glancing around fearfully, knees knocking. His mouth was open in a silent plea before he finally found his voice. "Please, sir, I hold proof."

Shaw waved his hand at his men. When they lowered their weapons, the fisherman continued to reach for his sporran and pulled out a golden ring of emerald and pearls. Shaw knew this ring. He'd given it to Jane as a gesture of friendship. A token of…his affection. He'd told her to send it if she ever needed him. When he'd told her he meant to collect on their debt, he'd never actually meant to take anything from the lass—other than perhaps convincing her when she was of age that she might like to grace his bed. It had taken a feat of pure willpower not to write her back when she'd said a life at sea would suit her to say he was coming to get her.

"Lady Marina," the fisherman said.

Marina… Jamarina… He let out a short laugh.

He'd not heard the name in a long time. It was the one he'd given her before she disembarked his ship. The lass had plagued his dreams for five long years. More beautiful than a woman had the right to be. He'd always felt guilty about his desire for her. For she'd been so young at the time, and pirate or nay, he had a code when it came to women. But not anymore. Now she'd be a woman grown, and the curves he'd felt when he carried her aboard his ship would have blossomed.

Shaw grunted and went back to the letter, the women on the floor pawing at his boots all but forgotten.

Dear Gentle Warrior,

I am prepared to pay my debt straightaway. 'Tis most urgent that you come now. Else, the balance will never be repaid, for there are others who wish to lay claim to the treasure I alone possess. I trust that your desire for adventure and thirst for the greatest of prizes will allow you to make haste to me. And know that I do not flatter myself that any sense of honor would bring you forth.

Most urgently yours in debt,

Lady M

"When did she give ye this?" Shaw demanded. The man stank of fish, his face the color and texture of dried leather.

"Early this morning, my laird. When I dropped off the fish at the abbey."

Shaw grunted. "And what was your payment for daring to step foot on my island?" He kept his voice calm, low, but it still had the power to cause the man to quake.

"The ring, sir."

"The ring," Shaw mused. He held the emerald jewel up to the candlelight. "So ye'll be wanting it back?"

"I'd be happy to leave with my life." The man's knees knocked together.

Shaw grinned, baring all of his teeth as he did so. "I suppose ye would." He closed his fingers around the ring. "Go then. Afore I unleash my beasts to feed on your bones. Ye were never here. Ye never saw this place. If anyone so much as lands on my beach by accident, I will hunt ye down and kill ye."

The old man nodded violently, then turned and ran toward the wide double doors that made up the entrance to Shaw's keep.

"Wait," Shaw called and two of his crew stepped in front of the old man to bar him from leaving. "Ye forgot something."

Trembling visibly, the fisherman turned, and Shaw tossed

him the ring. But his reflexes, or his nerves more like, weren't expecting it, and the ring fell to the stone before his feet. There was a measure of held breath in the air, and Shaw wondered if the man would pick it up or if the moments would tick by to the appropriate count that his men knew meant free game for whatever treasure had been dropped.

Seeming to understand the urgency, or perhaps just wishing to get the hell of Shaw's island, the fisherman scooped up the ring.

But instead of rushing out, he asked, "What should I tell my lady?"

"Ye needn't tell her anything," Shaw said. "I'll be there before ye get the chance."

With that, he blew a whistle to assemble a small crew and marched past the old fisherman, thinking at the last second to grab him by the scruff and drag him down to the docks before he was robbed for having overstayed his welcome.

Soon Shaw would lay his gaze on the beautiful lass again. Only this time, she would be a woman. Had the years at the abbey done her well? Was she now a child of God as she'd often struggled with deciding upon in her letters? And if she was, would he have the ballocks to corrupt her?

At that thought, Shaw laughed aloud as he gripped the helm.

Of course, he would.

He was Shaw Savage MacDougall. He took what he wanted, when he wanted. And never had he shied from debauching a willing woman.

Better yet was the question regarding what was this prize she claimed to possess? This treasure that he would not be able to resist?

He imagined a mountain of jewels and gold. A key to the king's own treasure stores. But truth be told, those were not the treasures he'd been pining over for years since last seeing her. Nay, the treasure he wanted was *her*.

In just a few hours time, he'd know what it was she was offering.

"Where to, Cap'n?" Jack asked, eagerness in his eyes.

"Iona."

Jack frowned. "Ain't nothing there we want, Cap'n."

Shaw turned a fierce glower on his crewman. "There is indeed something I want there. And ye best not be telling me again what it is I want, else I'll have ye hanging from the jack and make good on your name."

"Aye, Cap'n. Willna overstep again."

Shaw growled. "Make certain no one else does, either."

CHAPTER THREE

*A*s dawn approached, Jane climbed the bell tower, sat on the small bench and gazed out one of the arched belfry openings that looked toward the sea. Saints, but she hoped and prayed that at some point she'd see the black sails of MacDougall's ship coming through the fog off the Firth of Lorn.

The gentle sound of the waves lapping and the slight breeze that blew through the bell tower coupled with sheer exhaustion lulled her into a state close to sleep. She huddled deeper into her cloak and let her eyelids droop to half slits, still managing to keep a partial view of the sea.

"Come for me, gentle warrior," she murmured.

Jane didn't know how much time had passed, but in the courtyard below, she watched the sisters file into the nave. She knew they would wonder where she was, but she didn't having the energy to join them, or the nerve to leave this perch in case she missed the approach of his ship.

And then she saw them—the unforgettable darkened sails of the *Savage of the Sea*. One prominent sail was ruddy in color and had a massive ship painted on it with the image of a devil's head with a sword-bearing fist crushing it.

He'd come for her.

Jane sat up taller, her eyes suddenly wide and all remnants of sleep gone from her as renewed energy flowed rampantly. She made her way to the narrow ladder and climbed down from the bell tower, passing the nun whose duty it was to ring the bell for lauds.

"What is it?" she asked, taking in the urgency in Jane's darting gaze.

"I must go," was all Jane managed to say, her breathing quick.

Down in the cloister, the sisters of Iona walked from the refectory where they'd broken their fast and prepared for lauds in the nave. None seemed to notice as she passed going in the opposite direction, as it wasn't uncommon to see Jane —or rather *Marina*—wandering around at all hours and going in any manner of direction.

When she reached the wide double doors that locked them into their sanctuary, she felt the biting grip of her aunt's fingers on her arm.

"What are ye doing, child?" Aunt Agatha whispered, her brown eyes bright with concern, face pale in the dawn light. The too-tight wimple on her head made her skin taut at the edges.

"He has come for me, Aunt. Have faith, I will be safe."

"Who has come?" Agatha's brow tried to wrinkle beyond the tight wimple.

For a moment, Jane considered not telling her aunt and just demanding to be let go. Shaw had come for her, and if she didn't meet him out on the beach, who was to say he wouldn't come knocking on the abbey doors in search of her. After all, she had bribed him with treasure. "My protector."

"God is your protector, child."

Jane struggled with how to answer, for she'd never negate her aunt's beliefs. But she was fairly certain that when Livingstone came brandishing a sword, she would not be spared. "God protects us all, aye, my aunt, but he canna protect me from who comes. Not like Savage can." Oh, no! She'd not meant to let that name slip out.

"Savage? What kind of name is that?" Her aunt gasped, covering her mouth with her hand as understanding dawned. "Nay, lass. Ye canna mean…a pirate?"

It was too late to go back on what she'd said. Besides, all her aunt had to do was look outside the abbey walls and she'd see the swift approach of the pirate ship. And it was obviously a pirate ship. "Aye, Aunt Agatha. He is the one who brought me to Iona. He saved my life. And he is the only one who can save me now."

Aunt Agatha's face lost much of its piety in that moment as her eyes burned with protective rage. "Nay! I forbid it. I canna let ye go with a man who would destroy ye. I have sworn an oath to protect ye, to keep ye here. I told your father—"

"What did ye tell my father?"

"Nothing." Agatha glanced away.

All this time, Jane had thought her father believed her dead. She'd wanted him to think she was dead. Because if he believed her alive, if he knew where she was, then he could be tortured into giving the information away.

"Aunt! How could ye? He will be in danger!"

"From a pirate."

"Nay! From the men who killed the Earl of Douglas. The same ones who want me dead."

"Your father does not believe ye're here. He believes ye safely in Rome."

"Rome?"

"Aye. I told him we sent ye there."

Well, that was something at least.

"Please, dinna go with that pirate. He will be the death of ye."

"He will not, Aunt. But Livingstone…" Jane shuddered, and just from that gesture, understanding once more dawned in her aunt's eyes. "I've said too much. 'Tis better if ye know naught. Let me go, and dinna despair. Savage saved me once before, and he will do so again. I swear to ye. I will be safe."

But her aunt was shaking her head, her lips trembling as she stared at Jane as though she'd never seen her before.

"He will ruin ye. He will drag ye down into a life a crime. Ye'll be shunned by all. Shunned by God. Excommunicated. He is a devil."

MacDougall's brethren were known as the Devils of the Deep, and he was the prince of their fleet, but would the devil have brought her to God's house? She doubted it. Despite the rough exterior, the vicious reputation, there was something more to Shaw "Savage" MacDougall than met the eye. She could feel it.

"And ye'd rather see me dead? Because if I stay here, I'll be dead and buried within the week."

Tears gathered in Agatha's eyes, and she tugged Jane into her embrace, trembling as she held her.

"Pray for me, Aunt Agatha." And with that, she wrenched up the bar on the doors and ran through the opening, knowing that this was perhaps the last time she'd see her aunt, as Mother Superior would not allow her back once she knew the truth of where Jane had gone.

The moors were damp with dew that seeped into her sturdy leather boots, and then her feet were sinking into cool sand. The ship had laid anchor some distance out, but even in the dawn light she could see a skiff being rowed toward shore, and standing in the center of it was MacDougall himself.

The man's balance had to be impeccable, his strength evident. For who could stand so stoic on small boat like that?

He seemed taller than she remembered. Broader somehow. He wore a plaid of dark reds, golds and deep green almost black, a leine of black wool, and weapons that gleamed in the dawning pink light. His wild black hair blew in the wind and bronzed skin glistened in the glowing sun. In five years, she'd somehow shrunken him in her mind, lessened his roguish good looks. A mistake, for he was more mesmerizing than ever.

Jane's heart lurched. Her breath ceased, and her legs were suddenly wobbly. Had she made a mistake? Would he offer her protection in exchange for the secrets she kept? Or would he ravish her as her mind was now conjuring up all sorts of...

Get a hold of yourself, Jane!

What if her aunt was right, and he truly was a devil? What if him helping her before was only a single chance? What if...? Saints, there were so many questions darting back and forth in her head she was growing weary and dizzy.

She wanted to sit and catch her breath, or at least figure out how to breathe again. But to do so would be to show weakness, and the only thing she knew he despised more than Livingstone was weakness.

If she didn't stand tall and steady in what she wanted and needed, it would only allow him entry to walk all over her.

And she *would* get what she needed—his protection.

So Jane stood tall, hands on her hips, chin jutted, as she waited for him to arrive on the beach. The men chanted as they rowed, and then before she could turn around and run back to the sanctuary of Iona's abbey walls, the skiff was sliding up onto the beach and MacDougall was stepping down into the water, his large leather boot sinking into the sand and leaving a footprint the size of a crater. Their eyes met for an instant, and time stood still. She remembered those well. Emerald green and piercing. The way he was looking at her, as though he would devour her whole, made her limbs tingle, and she nearly faltered in her purposeful stance.

With deliberate intent, he marched toward her. Long, muscular legs with naked knees peeking from beneath his plaid. She jerked her gaze back up to his face to see that his eyes had darkened, and he either didn't like her perusal, or he liked it very much. It was hard to tell.

Oh, heaven help her… She didn't remember him being so…tall and large.

Or handsome.

Dark, wavy hair blew in the breeze and his face held a day or two's worth of stubble. When last she'd seen him, he'd a beard covering most of his face. Now she could make out the square jaw, the wide, intimidating mouth, a distinguished nose that had been broken at least twice, and his eyes… She felt he could see straight into her soul. If he were the devil, he'd know just what she was willing to sell her soul to him for.

"My lady, Ja—Marina," he said, voice full of confidence, a wry smile on his lips, as he swept a mocking bow and took her hand, bringing it close to his mouth.

A gentleman would brush the knuckles, or hover over the skin without making contact. But Savage was no gentleman. He pressed his lips firmly to the bare skin of her knuckles and left them there a hair's breadth longer than was appropriate, enough so that she felt a shiver skid from that spot straight to her belly.

Jane swallowed hard and snatched her hand back. "Ye made good time."

"Aye," he said slowly, taking his time as he raked his

intense gaze over her body. "I am most eager to collect my debt."

"And ye shall." She cleared her throat. "Now, if ye will, take me aboard your ship."

Her gentle warrior did not look so gentle now. He towered over her, his breadth blocking out the rising sun. There was a low rumble in his chest she thought might have been a laugh, and judging by the curl of his sensual mouth when he said, "Nay," she believed she was right.

Whatever game he was about, she wasn't interested in joining in. She cocked her head to the side and narrowed her eyes. "Ye would deny the treasure?"

"I would deny having ye aboard my ship." He let go of her hand then, but his gaze still held her taut enough she might as well have been pressed up against him.

"Then ye shall not collect your debt." Her nerves were so unamused, her heart leapt up into her throat, and she feared she might just start gagging.

"Lass, dinna trifle with me." He spoke low, menacingly, reaching forward to tuck her hair behind her ear.

"I would never dare trifle with a devil," she offered back, keeping herself steady.

He grinned. "Just as much spark as I remember. Now where is my treasure?"

"The treasure is up here." She tapped her head, surprised at the strength in her voice. "And I will only share it with ye, if ye take me aboard your ship."

"That is not how it works, lass."

Jane frowned. This was going to be a lot more difficult than she'd imagined. "Walk with me, MacDougall."

She didn't wait for him to answer. Instead, she turned on her heel and marched up the beach. With his legs easily two hands longer than hers, he quickly caught up.

"I dinna like to be bossed around by anyone, let alone a mere slip of a lass."

Jane let out a long sigh. "Please accept my apologies, sir. I am…" She wasn't any good at this—figuring out just how to appeal to a man to entice him into helping her. Perhaps the best course would be to simply be honest. "I am in need of your help in escaping this island. In exchange, I am willing to share with you information that has until now been known only to me and a select few others."

"Information?" The teasing turn of his lip lowered into a frown, and when next he spoke, it was not without warning. "Ye alluded to a treasure, lass. Dinna tell me ye've been lying."

She shook her head quickly. "Nay. I'm not lying. The information *leads* to a treasure. Call me the map."

"Ye deliberately misled me." She thought he might be angry, but his tone appeared more amused than anything else.

Jane chewed her lower lip, peeking up at him through her lashes, trying to gauge just how mad he might be. Aye, she'd spent some time with him, exchanged a few letters, but… perhaps she'd underestimated the bond they'd formed. He was a pirate, after all. And men of his ilk saw only gold and jewels when they looked at the world around them. "I told ye what ye needed to hear in order to get ye to come to Iona. But I didna mislead ye. 'Tis the greatest treasure in Scotland."

His eyes narrowed for a moment, and she thought he might say something more, but in the end he just said, "Tell me."

"Promise to take me away from Iona." This time, she didn't hide the hint of desperation in her voice, and she glanced over his shoulder for added emphasis.

"Why?" Real concern etched in his face giving her cause to believe that the bond they'd formed was true.

Jane gave him her full gaze then, rather than glancing

down at the sand or looking through her lashes. "Living-stone. He's coming for me."

While his expression did not change, there was a subtle pulse at his jaw as though he'd clenched his teeth, a flicker of something in his eyes. "I see."

"He is coming to kill me." Unbidden tears threatened, and she managed to hold them at bay.

Again, there was that flicker in his eyes, and she swore his arm twitched as though he wanted to reach for her. Oh, how she longed to sink against him, to feel the warmth of him. One night when they were on the ship, she'd fallen asleep beside him reading. When she woke, she realized he'd not moved, instead he'd just held her. How she'd cherished that moment for the past five years.

"How can ye be certain?"

His question brought her back to the present. "Mother Superior announced to us yesterday that we'd have special guest—Livingstone. That he was on a pilgrimage across the country. But I know he is looking for me."

"Because he wants ye dead?"

"Aye."

"Because ye were there at the death feast." He stated it rather than asking.

"Partly. But also because of what I know." She ran her hands through her hair and looked down at their boots sinking into the sand. "If only I were not so...stupid."

"Lass?"

She flashed a bitter smile at him. "I shouldna have goaded William into telling me. Then I could be blissfully ignorant of it all."

"But he would still be coming for ye, and then ye'd have nothing to barter with to get ye off the island." Then his dark gaze roved over her body in a way that sent shivers rolling through her. "Well, almost nothing."

She gasped, catching his meaning, and took a step back. "Ye're a—"

"Devil?" he interrupted, stepping closer. "Aye, lass, I am, and it seems ye're willing to negotiate with me. 'Haps I dinna want whatever secrets ye hold, but instead I want...*ye*."

"I am not a pawn," she shouted, feeling anger slice through her. "I am through being a pawn."

The devil had the gall to laugh at that. All the fairytale apparitions floating before her eyes whipped from her mind faster than the lash on a pirate's back.

"We shall see, Ja-Marina. Now, tell me your secret, and I will let ye know if it is worth the price of this gentle warrior taking ye off this island."

He was mocking her. The cad. But what other choice did she have? It wasn't as if she could get off the island on her own. If she bribed the fisherman into taking her away, he might only ask for what the pirate had alluded to, and she was definitely not willing to give away her own precious gifts to the old man.

"Last month, Joan Beaufort, mother of the king, was killed in a siege at Dunbar castle. A siege laid upon them by Livingstone."

"I had heard."

"She sustained injuries in the battle, from which she died. But her husband, James Stewart, the Black Knight of Lorne, was able to escape with their children and his page."

"This is common knowledge, lass. Ye'll have to do better than that."

Jane nodded, twisting her fingers together. "The page was not his *page*."

"His squire? His cook?" Savage chuckled. "I hope ye've got something more interesting than that, love."

"He was *Alexander*."

At this, MacDougall frowned, his face darkening. "Alexander who?"

"Alexander Stewart, Duke of Rothesay, the eldest twin born on the sixteenth of October, year of our Lord 1430."

Shaw's scowl darkened. "The king's twin, the elder twin? The one who died that day?"

Jane shook her head. "He did not die."

"He did, my lady. Someone has fed ye a pack of lies, and now ye're trying to sell them to me."

"I am not lying." But she did wonder if perhaps she had been told a lie herself. "William told me before he died that the Black Knight had a page who was the spitting image of the king. That the page, was in fact, the rightful king. 'Tis why Livingstone wanted my husband and his brother dead. Because they knew and could replace the puppet Livingstone is manipulating. Now he wants me dead. But not before he tortures the truth from me."

"What truth? If ye know this, than he likely does, too."

Jane shook her head. "He will want me dead for more than that. Livingstone…" She chewed her lip again, finding her throat tight. "I know the truth about where James and Alexander, the true king, are hiding."

"How could ye know this?"

Locking her eyes on Shaw, she said, "Because, they came here seeking sanctuary. Because I told them where to go."

"And Livingstone knows they were here?"

"Aye."

"How?"

"Sister Maria."

Shaw raised a brow.

"She came back, I wrote to ye of this. But after Lorne and Alexander's visit, she left swiftly again. And now we've had word that Livingstone comes. I think she was a spy."

At this final admission, the pirate opened his mouth and

then closed it again. She might not have believed she could make him speechless if she hadn't witnessed it herself.

"And where did ye tell them to hide, love?" His voice was soft, emerald eyes glittering.

"That I willna tell ye until ye let me onboard your ship. Until ye offer me protection."

He grinned, but it wasn't one filled with mirth, more like that of a pirate who'd just glimpsed his treasure and knew it would soon be his.

"There is only one way I will offer ye protection, love." His grin took on a sensual curve.

Jane squared her shoulders, thrust her chin forward. "Name your price."

"Ye…in my bed."

Jane felt as though a gale force wind had knocked her back. He would take her information and her body? "Nay." She watched his face darken and decided that perhaps another type of bargain could be hatched between them. "I shall agree to a…kiss, but nothing more."

A brow winged up at that. "I'm a pirate, lass. I dinna claim anything without fully possessing it—including a woman."

Another wayward shiver passed through her. Why did her body keep doing that? Why did that heated gaze he tossed at her have places on her body tingling that she didn't know *could* tingle? Jane swallowed hard. Was there any other choice? Perhaps she could accept his terms, with an addendum of her own. "All right, but there is only one way I'll ever enter your bed, *gentle warrior*."

His eyes glittered like sparkling jewels. "Name your price, lass."

Jane lifted her chin, meeting his gaze head on, and not wavering in the least. "Marriage."

CHAPTER FOUR

*S*haw let out a ruthless laugh. The lass was jesting, wasn't she? "Marriage? Love do ye know who ye're talking to?"

Jane's chin jutted forward, and though she was staring up at him, the glare she fixed him with made him think she was looking down her nose at him. "I know *exactly* who I am speaking with."

A little taken aback, the grin he held faltered. She *was* serious. "Then what on earth would possess ye to propose marriage, love?" Bedding her, aye, but marriage? To hell with that.

"Propose." She huffed and turned in a circle, running her hands through her lustrous hair, her frustration clear and damned confusing.

To say he was stunned by what the lass had relayed and her subsequent request for a wedding would be an understatement, but Shaw wasn't about to let her in on that. Especially not if he could get her to change her mind about the wedding part and still get her in his bed in the process. Marriage was definitely off the table, though.

She needed his protection, there was no doubt of that. And he'd be willing to bet she'd give almost anything to have it. He was probably the only man in Scotland willing to thwart that bastard Livingstone. And she knew it.

Smart lass.

If what she'd told him about Alexander and the fact that she knew his whereabouts was true, Livingstone would not let her go until the breath had left her body. That whoreson would chase them both to the ends of the earth, for it seemed she was the only one who could bring down the entire kingdom, until Alexander was of an age to do so himself. The lad would be about fifteen now, and if the Black Knight who protected him was smart, he'd wait until the boy king was at least twenty-one summers before pushing him to rise up against his own twin brother.

Jane stared him down now, daring him to deny her. How was it that this little slip of a lass could make him question his entire pirate code?

With a sigh, he hoped she couldn't hear, he asked, "When is Livingstone supposed to arrive?"

"Any day now," she murmured, looking over his shoulder again. "Maybe even any hour." A myriad of emotions flitted over her face. Sadness, guilt, despair. And not once did he see hope.

Why did that bother him? Why did he care if she had any hope?

Bloody hell, he had no idea why he cared. But the truth was, he did. It was why he'd written her back when he got her letters. Possibly the reason why he'd felt slightly bereft when their letters had to cease. Shaw cleared his throat, pushing away his weakening thoughts. By the rood, he was a bloody pirate prince! He didn't let silly lassies and their even sillier hopes and dreams get in the way of where he was headed.

Stick to the basics, he told himself. Bedding her would be a most treasured gift.

Triton's trident, but she'd grown into a beautiful, luscious woman, just as he'd expected her to. She was lush and curvy in all the right places. Breasts that pushed the confines of her humble gown, hips that flared and a waist that was lost in the ridiculously pious garment, but he bet he could span it with both hands. Her long blond locks radiated gold, and her blue eyes were more beautiful than a summer sky and had deeper depths than the sea he loved so much. Blast, he couldn't stop looking at her mouth. Plush red lips that would feel decadent pressed to his. They could make him give up everything if she put them somewhere else.

Devil take it! "Then we must leave now." His tone brooked no argument.

"Not until ye agree." Her hands were back on those curvy hips, right where he wanted to touch to pull her close, to massage the voluptuous swells.

Shaw raised a brow, feeling his body tighten. "My, my. Back to bossing around the big bad pirate, are we?"

She huffed and crossed her arms over her chest, which only served to push those plump breasts up higher. "I dinna see that I have any other choice, *Savage.*"

His grin widened, and he tried hard not to stare at the wares she showed off so well. "Neither do I. Well, that is, unless ye choose death." Shrugging, he tried to put off an air of not giving a damn. If she knew just how much she was affecting him, he'd be lost.

Those red lips parted on a gasp, then trembled. *Damn!*

"I dinna wish to die." Blue eyes implored him.

"And I dinna wish to be married, sweet Ja-marina."

She sniffed at him. "So we are at an impasse. Ye dinna want my treasure?"

Oh, that was a trap she'd laid, and he walked right into.

His gaze raked her, only making the tightening in his groin all the more uncomfortable. "Oh, lass, I want your *treasure* verra much."

Her eyes widened in innocent surprise, as if she'd not been trying to bait him. "The rightful king, ye wretch, *that* treasure."

Shaw chuckled. "Ye need not explain to me what ye meant. Ye've offered me many things, and I would have them all."

"Marriage?" She raised a challenging brow.

He grimaced. "Let us take that off the bargaining table."

"Then ye must take me *out* of your bed."

"I will *take* ye any place ye wish, love." God, he wanted to touch her. They were close enough, he could just reach forward a little and stroke her soft cheek, brush his thumb over her lower lip.

She rolled her eyes and let out a groan. "Ye know exactly what I mean, and yet ye toy with me. I need to get off this island. I'm willing to share with ye the greatest national treasure, and nothing else, unless ye put a ring on my finger and vow before the Lord and your crew that I am yours for eternity."

"All right."

She gasped. "All right?"

"I will put my ring on your finger, and I will vow before anyone who listens that ye are mine. And then I will take ye to bed and discover all of your secrets."

She narrowed her eyes. "I'm not certain that what ye said constitutes marriage."

"It does in the eyes of pirates and Scottish law."

If she kept worrying that lower lip, he was liable to take it between his own teeth and start nibbling.

"Then we are in agreement," she whispered.

"Are we?" He leaned closer, breathing in her sweet floral scent.

"Aye," she whispered, momentarily affected by his closeness. "Please, take me aboard your ship, MacDougall."

"My lady will not call me MacDougall or Savage."

"What should I call ye then, gentle warrior?"

"Not around my men. Call me Shaw. Or master if ye prefer." He snickered, unable to help goading her.

She rolled her eyes. "Shaw it is. And call me Jane."

"Not Ja--Marina?"

"I canna believe ye remembered that."

"Lass, I could never have forgotten ye."

At that, her eyes widened and her mouth formed a perfect little circle. Hell, he surprised himself by admitting it. There was only one way to make them both forget his blunder.

Shaw reached for her, settled his palm at the base of her spine and hauled her up to his frame, feeling all those lush curves pressed so tantalizingly against him.

"In my world, when a bargain is struck, it must be sealed." He eyes searched hers, pleased that there was hardly a hint of fear.

"And how do ye propose to seal this?" Jane's gaze flickered to his lips. "The same way ye seal other bargains with pirates?"

He chuckled. She wanted him, even if she refused to admit it. "Nay, love. Never that way. I'll show ye." And then his mouth was on hers, nibbling those plush lips like he'd wanted to, tasting the sweet succulence of her gloriously sensual mouth, and laying claim to what she offered. Innocent and tentative at first, she quickly grew bolder, imitating the slide of his tongue.

Oh, ballocks... She was heaven and hell all at the same time. Sweetness and fire. Kissing her had been a mistake. Agreeing to have her in his bed under the pretense of marriage was worse, for with that one kiss, he knew he'd never get enough of her. The touch of his lips to hers had awakened something inside him that should have been left undiscovered. But it wasn't. It was gaping and grasping.

She was consuming him.

And he couldn't pull away.

In fact, he wrapped his other arm around her and lifted her up off her feet, pressing his hard cock to the apex of her thighs so she would know just how much he desired her, so she would know just what she'd bargained for.

Jane was *his*. And so were all of her secrets.

No coherent thought other than she'd never been kissed like this before went through Jane's mind. She should slap him, push him away, at the very least demand to be put back on her own feet and a good measure of space put between them.

But she did none of those things. Instead, she found herself winding her arms around his neck, parting her lips and sighing against his demanding lips. The spicy-salty scent of him surrounded her, doing something wild to her senses. Suddenly, every part of her was alive with a tingling fire that only seemed ready to burn hotter.

Parting her lips seemed to be a wicked invitation, for as soon as she did it, his devious tongue swept along the open seam, causing her to gasp.

Oh sweet heavens, that felt even more divine. Just that little lick sent a jolt rushing through her. And before she could catch her wits, he'd done it again, and again, and then her own tongue was reaching forward to test it out. She touched the tip of her tongue to his and could have been struck by lightning, so massive was the force of current that went rushing through her.

This was wicked, oh, so very wicked. And yet, she couldn't make herself stop.

And did she have to? She'd given herself to this man. Had agreed to share his bed in exchange for him vowing she was his, a marriage that may end up being a total sham, for all she knew. But that didn't change the fact that she'd agreed to it, that in order to be saved from Livingstone, to keep the rightful king safe, she had invited this pirate to lay claim to her.

And lay claim to her, he was. There could be no doubt about the way he owned her body at that moment. She couldn't move. He had her completely enthralled. Completely captivated. Intoxicated.

It was he who pulled away first. He who stared into her bemused eyes with a satisfied expression that she would have found overly irritating if she wasn't so busy trying to find her bearings.

Shaw set her down on her feet and grinned at her as though he'd plucked a tart straight from her fingers and devoured it.

"I hope that satisfies your need," she murmured, "for sealing deals."

He chuckled then, a sound that caressed her nerves but did very little in the way of calming her. In fact, it did quite the opposite. She licked her lips, trying to avoid looking at his mouth as she very much wanted him to kiss her once more. He might have set her down on her feet, but she was barely standing on her own. Every line in her body reached for him, wanting more of what he'd just given her.

"That was just a taste, love, of what satisfies, but not nearly enough."

"Shall we do it again then?" she asked in challenge, and

then felt the heat rush to her face for having spoken so boldly.

Shaw's darkened gaze swept over her, daring and devilish, and right along with it, her body quivered. He wanted her. And she...wanted him.

"Oh, sweet Jane, we shall do it again many more times. But first—" He glanced back out at sea, and for the first time she noticed the two men sitting in the skiff. How could she have forgotten about them? "Let us get back to the ship, else we give your pursuer more chances to come and find ye."

She expected him to offer his arm as they turned on the beach to walk toward the rowboat, but he did not. Nor did he wait for her. Instead, he took off at a solid march, leaving her to trail behind.

Well, he was no gentleman, and he did not claim to be one. Trying hard not to pout at his brutish ways, she started to step forward when he turned and frowned at her.

"Are ye waiting for a gale, love?"

"What?" she asked, offended at his obvious remark on her pace, and irritated that he should go from kissing her to treating her like a bothersome pest.

"Come on then, we've not got all day."

Jane lifted the hem of her skirt and hurried forward until she was beside him. She clamped her mouth closed against any admonishment she might have made when he pressed his hand to the small of her back in a show of possession. When the lapping water of the shore touched the tips of her boots, he swept her up in his arms and carried her like a lover through the water to the skiff, depositing her in the center and stepping in behind her.

Perhaps there was a bit more gentleman in him than he cared to admit. That thought made her smile.

"Row," he ordered his men.

Jane gazed out toward the sea, refusing to turn around to

look at the abbey. She was afraid she'd see the disapproving looks of her aunt and the other women who she'd lived with. They'd cared for the last five years, and she in turn cared for them. Mother Superior had taken her in without any assurances that a dowry would be coming to pay her way. Mother Superior and Agatha, who'd kept her secrets.

And she could not give them anything, not even a pitiful farewell. For to tell them she was saving their lives by disappearing would be to give them too much. Better that they remain ignorant of Livingstone's crimes and the political upheaval that Jane herself had become embroiled in. Aunt Agatha would keep quiet about it, she was certain, not wanting to further ruin Jane's reputation and her own by association.

The passage over the water was quick, and at the base of the hull of the ship, Jane stared up at the vastness of wide wooden planks, cannon heads, steely pegs, rigging and sails. This ship was a powerful and mighty force in and of itself. She recalled how the last time she'd been aboard, she'd been so full of hope and fear. And now, she was boarding in much the same state.

"Up ye go, lass," Shaw said behind her. "Else ye want me to toss ye over my shoulder and carry ye."

"Nay," she said quickly, glancing back at him, afraid he might do just that. "I can manage."

She gripped the slippery, thick ropes and put her foot on the first rung, hoisting herself up. The climb up was harder than the climb down had been, but she managed it, not unused to putting her body to work. She'd done quite a bit of manual labor at the abbey and was pleased she'd not lain about idle like some other ladies who'd passed through.

At the top, Jack pulled her over the rail and grinned. He looked just as rascally as he had before. Roughly her height and thick with muscle, he had hair stiff from the salt and skin as brown as bread, eyes as dark as night, and a braided beard that reached his chest. "Welcome back, my lady."

Shaw leapt onto the deck beside her and pulled her roughly into his side, his arm slung over her shoulder. "Lady Jane has returned to us," he said to his crew. "She is to be my wife."

At that, the entire crew burst into uncontrollable laughter, and Jane felt her face heat to what the fires in Hell must truly feel like.

CHAPTER FIVE

a growl ripped from Shaw's throat that had the entire crew clamping their beaks firmly shut. "Laugh all ye like, ye landlubbers. But 'tis the truth." Shaw gripped both of Jane's hands in his, prepared to announce his vows to all standing before them when he realized they needed something to wrap their hands for the traditional handfast. "Jack, lend me your sleeve."

Jack ripped off his sleeve without question, wrenching the fabric free as though it were nothing. His soon-to-be wife flinched but didn't say a word.

"Wrap our hands," Shaw demanded of his quartermaster.

"Ye're serious, Cap'n." Jack's mouth was wide, as was the rest of the crew, and he looked as though he would say more, but Shaw fixed him with a look that said one more word would equal a deadly punishment.

The men from the boatswain, mates down to the lowliest swab, understood he was serious, and they grew silent as the grave.

"Aye." Shaw's voice rumbled low, threatening, and he felt

Jane's hands tremble in his. "Do it fast. We need to be on our way."

He returned his gaze to Jane, taking in her eyes flickering from the crew to him, creamy cheeks a shade paler. She looked as nervous as he felt, which irritated the bloody piss out of him. Why should he be nervous? Was he weakening already? It was only a handfast. As soon as he saw Livingstone into his grave, he'd part with the lass and tell her she need not worry about being tied to a pirate for the rest of her days. He'd set her free.

For she could not truly want a marriage with him. What lass would? Especially one who was born of noble blood and had been married before to an earl. She would be seeking out a better match if she wasn't in danger of losing her life. Indeed, if Livingstone had never found her, she'd still be safely tucked away in the abbey.

Besides, when the business was done, Shaw would have what he wanted—the lass in his bed and a pile of gold to keep the whereabouts of Alexander secret. He didn't care about the lad's position in Scotland. Shaw bowed to no king. What he did bow to was the power of gold. And with what she was giving him, he and his men could be set for a few years or more.

"Well?" He eyed Jack, who seemed to have frozen in place. "Get on with it."

Jack nodded so violently his hair came free of its queue. But he did what he was told, wrapping their hands in his torn sleeve. The tighter their hands were wrapped, the more Jane's trembling calmed. Interesting, because it only made his insides twist all the more.

Not one to dally, Shaw leapt right into it. "From this day forth, with this crew and the sea as our witnesses, I handfast myself to Lady Jane... What is your full name, love?"

"Jane Lindsay Douglas." Her voice was soft, just above a

whisper, and she blushed, glancing up at him through her lashes like a virginal bride, which he knew she couldn't be. She'd been married to a sixteen-year-old lad, and Shaw remembered being that age and just how randy he'd been.

"I hereby handfast myself to Lady Jane Lindsay Douglas, now Lady Savage." He winked at her gasp.

"And I…Lady Savage," she choked on this last word, "handfast myself to Shaw MacDougall, Prince of the Devils of the Deep." She closed her eyes, a visible shudder whipping through her.

Och, that was a knock to his pride.

"Relax, love, it may seem like ye've sold your soul to the devil, but I assure ye, I'm only a man."

Sparkling blue eyes blinked open to gape at him, trepidation in their depths. She nodded, though it was obvious she was only doing so out of pretense. No matter, their business would soon conclude and she'd be on her way, free to live her life away from him and his men.

"Ye may kiss your bride," Jack added, and the whistles went up around the ship.

Shaw grinned. He'd not miss an opportunity to kiss her again. The first time had been incredible. The second would be even better. Tugging her close by their joined hands, he bent down and swiped his lips over hers, feeling the way she trembled against him.

But it wasn't the kind of trembling he wanted in his woman. Jane was trembling from angst, not from pleasure or anticipation. That wouldn't do. He might be a dangerous and deadly pirate, but that didn't mean he wanted his woman to fear his touch.

Shaw wrenched their hands from the ties and cupped the side of her face, gently stroking. He gazed deep into her eyes, hoping to ease some of her distress. But it only served to make her tremble all the more.

Damned if that slight quake of worry didn't feel like a kick to his ballocks.

"Blast it," he muttered and turned away from her. He wanted to kiss her, not make her faint. "Jack, take her to my cabin. The rest of ye, all hands on deck! Set the sails, ready the masts. Away we go to Castle Dheomhan. From there, a new adventure awaits!"

His crew let out a cheer and went about their duties hoisting sails and working the rigging as they sang. Shaw gripped the helm, steering them away from Iona and back toward Scarba and the rest of his fleet. Kelly, Lachlan and Thor would be surprised as hell to find out he'd handfasted himself to a woman. Like his crew, they'd probably wonder what had gotten into him, question his mental capacity and possibly even his skill with a sword.

As they navigated away from the island, the stone abbey growing smaller, Shaw could make out the billowing white sails of an approaching ship. They were too far away to see exactly who it was, but if he were a betting man, and he was, he'd say it was Livingstone. They'd left in the knick of time. If he'd waited to come to Iona until the morning instead of sailing through the night, he'd have been too late. A sharp bristle of anger stabbed at his middle, and his insides twitched with the need to wrench the helm, turning the *Savage of the Sea* toward the blackguard. To order the canons loaded and to fire upon the bastard. But he didn't have his full crew on board, nor all his canons loaded, and Livingstone likely did.

Shaw supposed a battle to the death would have to wait for another day—but it *would* happen. That made him grin, for he loved nothing more than a good sea battle. And if anyone deserved to be beaten, it was that bloody whoreson. Shaw gave a mock solute to the distant ship and growled, "Scurvy dog."

"Cap'n?" Jack approached, glancing at the ship in the distance and then back at his captain at the helm.

"Aye, Jack?"

"The lass is in your quarters. Would ye be wantin' me to be taking the helm? Make the ceremony official?"

Shaw sneered. Aye, he wanted. He wanted to head to his quarters and show the lass just what a pirate's pleasure was, but instead, he growled at his quartermaster and then looked back out to sea. The rest of the crew was looking at him as though he'd lost his mind, though discreetly as they worked, and he couldn't be having that. They already probably thought him mad for having wed in the first place. If he didn't then go make the lass his fully, they'd start to doubt his sincerity as a man, as a pirate, as their prince.

"Bloody hell. Take it, Jack," he demanded, and then stormed across the deck, punching one of the swabs as he went for daring to gape too much.

The lad went flying, one of the boatswains grabbing his hand before he sailed overboard. The men cheered, seeming to have gotten their confidence in him back quickly enough.

Shaw stomped up the steps to his cabin and burst through the door. Jane leapt a foot from where she stood staring at his overstuffed bookcases. When she turned to face him, he felt her gaze like a punch to the gut. With his foot, he kicked the door closed behind him, drowning out the cheers of the crew.

"I wondered how long it would take ye to come to me." She lifted her chin, challenging. The blue of her eyes were piercing, and he found himself wanting to look away.

What was it about her that made him feel like that? As though she could see deep into his soul and know his fears, lay them out before him. He was a man who never doubted, never shrank, but in her presence, he felt reduced somehow. Weak. It was quite vexing.

"A wife should not speak to her husband like that, let alone one as dangerous as me." Shaw's tone was low as he slowly advanced on her.

To his pleasure, she didn't seem at all affected. Quite the opposite, in fact. She tipped a shoulder and glanced at him as playfully as she had when she'd been in his cabin five years before. "If ye're a pirate prince, does that make me a princess?"

He chuckled. "Doesna work that way."

"Hmm." She turned back to the books and slid her fingers over the titles. "Ye've added quite a few things to your cabin since the last time I was here."

"Aye. Plundering is my passion." Shaw approached her from behind and pressed his hands to her hips, possessive. She wobbled but didn't pull away. If anything, she leaned a fraction of an inch backward. Was that permission? He leaned forward, breathing in the sweet, floral scent of her hair and pressed his lips to the delicate shell of her ear. "Do ye know what comes next?"

Jane sucked in a ragged breath when he darted his tongue out to tease the sensitive flesh behind her ear, and she whispered, "Aye."

She'd been married before, nearly raped when he first found her. Of course, she knew what happened between a man and a woman.

"Turn around." Though a demand, his voice was remarkably soft, surprising even himself.

Obediently, Jane turned to face him, her eyes squarely on his chest, and a lovely blush creeping over her creamy skin. God, he wanted to lick every inch of her.

"Look at me." With two fingers on her chin, he gently encouraged her to tilt her head up.

Again, she did as he demanded without argument, her eyes piercing into his. *Blast it!* Why did she have to look at him like that? Half-fearful, half-resigned—and yet there was a curiosity buried deep in that fear and resignation. Whatever her apprehensions were, she was interested in what would happen.

That was encouraging. Enough to make him stay. If she looked at him like she had when he kissed her on deck, he wouldn't be able to go through with what he truly desired. Dread wasn't what he wanted in a bedmate. He'd never taken a woman against her will, and he wasn't about to start now. But he would have her. And willing she'd be. If there was one thing he was good at, it was gifting the lasses bountiful rapture. He knew she'd liked it when he kissed her on the beach. Knew she'd trembled then from pleasure, desire.

Shaw stroked the hair away from her temple, tucking it behind her ear, never letting his eyes leave hers.

Leaning forward, he brushed his lips over hers at the same time he slid his fingers over the length and curve of her collarbone. Neither of them closed their eyes, gazes locked in a battle for who would submit first. With her quick inhale of breath against his mouth, his blood immediately rushed hot and heavy through his veins and straight to his cock. Trailing his fingers over the column of her neck, he caressed her lightly, teasingly as he continued to kiss her with gentle persistence.

Shaw wanted to see every reaction, to gauge whether she liked what he was doing and to finally see her surrender. She, he suspected, was working hard to keep her sharp and steady resolve. To keep this a simple vowed transaction.

With his other hand, Shaw ran his fingers up and down her spine, feeling her muscles ease with each stroke. Each stone defense she'd erected, he was taking down with one touch and slide of his lips. Slowly, he backed her toward the bookcases she seemed so enamored with, and when her bottom hit the wood, he pressed his hard body fully against her luscious curves, swallowing back a groan at the gasp on her lips. Triton's trident, but full body contact felt damned good. All he had to do was lift his plaid, lift her skirts and then that wicked, wet heat would be his. Shaw did groan then, imagining sinking deep inside her, Jane's legs wrapped around his hips. If he kept this up, he'd come before he got there.

Her eyelids fluttered and then widened as she worked to keep control of the situation.

Rather than deepen the kiss, Shaw freed her lips from his, but only to grasp her hand and bring that upward to kiss each fingertip. Her mouth pressed into a tight line, but the rapid rise and fall of her chest, as well as the way her eyes twitched, were telltale signs that he was getting to her.

"Surrender," he whispered, taking one of her fingers into his mouth and gently flicking it with his tongue before sucking.

She let out a little cry and tried to tug her finger away, but he only sucked harder, pinning her to the bookcase with his hips. The hardness of his arousal tucked tightly at the crux of her thighs. When she wriggled, it was a pure delicious torment.

Dipping to kiss her again, he whispered. "Ye will have me undone, love."

Eyes widening, she glanced down at where their bodies were joined, a naïve understanding lighting her eyes. This woman had been married. Aye, she'd been a child, but she must have…

Och, she couldn't be a virgin. Just unused to the wooing of man since she'd only been married to a boy. Oh, aye, there was much he could teach her about the loving between a man and a woman.

"There is much pleasure to be shared," he said, letting her

finger go and leaning down to press his lips to her neck where her pulse leapt. "So much pleasure."

Her heartbeat quickened.

"Do ye like it when I kiss ye?" he asked.

"Aye," she answered without hesitation. "Nay."

"Which is it?" he teased, nipping her jaw.

She sighed. "It *should* be nay."

"But it isna."

"Nay."

Shaw chuckled, taking her earlobe between his teeth and gently tugging, as he gently rocked his hips back and forth. "Tell me what ye want."

She sucked in a breath, tilting her head to the side. "I want ye to leave me alone."

Those were not the words he'd expected to hear, and indeed, they did take him by surprise, for as she said it, she clutched his shirt and let out a soft gasp. With her words, she was saying nay, but with her body, she was very much saying aye.

"I will leave ye if that is your wish." He skimmed his tongue over her jaw, then over toward her mouth where he captured her lips in a possessive kiss.

The kiss was hot, deep, and if he were a true bastard, he would have ignored her words, lifted her skirts and taken her right there against the books. But as much as he wished he was a true blackguard at that moment, he simply couldn't take advantage of her. She wanted him, her body couldn't lie. Tight, pointy nipples pressed through her gown to tease his chest, but as much as he wanted to, he wouldn't touch them, not until she begged.

"Aye," she moaned. "Leave me. Please."

Shaw stepped back with a groan at the cool air that replaced her sweet heat.

The front of his plaid jutted out with the hard length of

him. He scraped his hands through his hair, and then swiped them over his face, close to shaking with his rampant need. Damn, but he'd never wanted a woman as much as he wanted Jane. Never been this physically affected. It was mind-blowing.

"A drink?" he asked gruffly, clearing his throat.

"Aye," she said, letting out the breath she'd been holding. Her gaze raked over the length of him, widening as she took in the bulge of his plaid. She licked her lips, eyes still hazy with desire, and it took every bit of willpower not to reach for her again.

Even now, her nipples were still two delicious points pushing through the softness of her plain gown. The garment was not meant to entice in the least. A dull brown, and threadbare in spots, it came all the way up to her neck and did nothing to flatter the curves he'd felt beneath. But it didn't matter, at this moment, the damned thing was the most erotic piece of clothing he'd ever laid eyes on—and he'd seen all manner of silks and lace on the wenches at his pirate ports.

Tearing his gaze away, he walked to his liquor cabinet. "Whisky?"

"I've never had one," she said. "But it seems appropriate at this moment."

Shaw chuckled. "Aye, love, that it does."

CHAPTER SIX

A few hours later, the sun shone brightly through the porthole, centering on Jane where she sat in the exact spot she'd taken up when Shaw offered her whisky before leaving the cabin. He'd not been back to her relief and her despair. She was warmer, perhaps a bit tipsy, but still a maiden.

Aye, though she'd been married, a consummation of the marriage had never occurred. Not for lack of desire on William's part. But their marriage contract said they were to wait for a certain date, which when it came to pass found her indisposed, and then they'd traveled to Edinburgh. As a result, she was still *virgo intacta*. And if she had her way, she would remain that way. But only if Shaw did not kiss her like that again. Because no matter how hard she'd tried to hold out, before he'd stopped, she'd been ready to shed her gown and give him everything he seemed so intent on gaining.

She let out a shuddering breath as she stared at the door, the same thing she'd been doing since he'd left her to go up on deck. At any moment, she'd expected him to come back into the cabin and make good on his promises of pleasure.

Truth be told, there was still a part of her that was ready and willing to allow him. The way he'd kissed her, touched her, had felt *so* incredibly good.

The more rational side of her head reminded her, rather logically, that if she could just satisfy him with kisses, then he would take care of Livingstone and she could be on her way.

They'd only handfasted. And she knew how very temporary a handfasting could be. Also, if she were still a maiden, she would be that much more appealing to a man who actually wanted to wed her. The thought of marriage, however, left her with a sour taste in her mouth. Her first marriage had been disappointing, and this second one, if it could be counted, would be dangerous. She was tired of being a pawn in the games of men, which is what would happen if she were to marry someone else. After this was over, she'd have to go home to her father, as he would expect such, and he'd sell her off to the next man in want of a wife.

The realization made her belly roll. Maybe it would be best to give in to Shaw. To let him take the bargaining chip her father could use away. Besides that, no respectable man would want to bed down with a woman who'd lain with a notorious pirate.

But if she did give in... And, oh, how that wicked part of her wanted to, then Shaw would forever *own* her. Even if they did separate, how could she ever forget the way he kissed, the way he owned her with the swipe of his tongue? It would be that much worse if he entered her body.

Jane rubbed at her eyes and let out a frustrated groan. So, no, she could not allow him to finish what they'd started.

She was in way over her head. The man was a master of seduction, and at least a half-dozen times when he'd been kissing her, she'd been one heart-stopping breath away from utter surrender.

The door swung open, sending the hem of her skirts to

ruffle with the sudden disruption of air. Jane gasped, hands falling to her sides, belly falling to her feet.

Shaw stopped on the threshold, as if he'd not expected to see her there waiting. The man was magnificent, and huge, taking up the entire expanse of the doorway. That dark, billowy shirt clung to the muscles of his upper body. A slight V of skin where the laces at his throat had come undone exposed tanned skin. Dark hair pulled into a queue. Mouth in a firm line. Glittering, heated emerald gaze that swept her from head to toe. Saints, she felt like he was stripping her bare with that one intense stare.

Heat washed over her, and it could have been only a few moments that he was gone for all her body recalled exactly how his hard one felt on her. "Shaw." She blew out a breath.

He cleared his throat, dragging his eyes from her legs to her eyes. "We've arrived."

"At your castle."

"My island." His chest puffed a little bit.

She clasped her hands, hoping that squeezing them together would help her to still their trembling. "Your own island?"

"Aye. Scarba. 'Tis mine."

On shaky legs, she stood and strode toward him. "I am ready."

He raised a brow, gaze darkening with desire and falling to her lips.

"To debark the ship," she clarified.

He let out a soft chuckle, but his eyes still held the intensity of a man filled with hunger.

She might be a maiden, but it wasn't as though she'd not witnessed that look before. Even on wee William. But Livingstone had intervened before they were able to move forward with their marital obligations, and brutally cut short William's life.

As much as an arrogant child as he'd been, she had not wished him dead.

"What are ye thinking of?" Shaw studied her, and she realized she'd been frowning.

Jane wiped her face clean of her thoughts and worked a troubled smile from her lips. "I was just thinking about the last time I was brought to the home of a husband."

"Do ye miss him?"

That was not a question she'd expected to hear from Shaw, and she decided to be honest. "Nay, but I didna wish him dead."

He nodded, not seeming to need anything more, then swept his arm out indicating they should leave. Jane took the narrow stairs first, with Shaw behind her. She could feel his gaze on her, heating her, and she couldn't help but notice the sway of her own hips and tried to cease the movement as she walked. Oh, why did women have to be cursed with hips?

At the bottom of the stairs, her face was sufficiently reddened she was certain, not only from the heat of her cheeks, but also the bawdy cheers the men gave, clearly thinking their prince had kissed the breath out of her— among other things.

Jane jerked her gaze toward the ground, but then Shaw took hold of her elbow and whispered. "I know ye're no weak lass, and they need to know it, too. Ye're their mistress, their pirate princess, love."

She jerked her head up then, staring at each of the men as they passed toward the starboard side and the wood-planked gangway that had been lowered leading to the dock.

The men tipped their hats and bowed their heads as she passed. As debauched and ferocious as they appeared, the feeling of excitement and pride that filled her chest was like none she'd ever had. When she'd arrived at the Douglas home years ago, she'd been a meek, head-bowed bride, and so they had always treated her that way. Shaw was giving her permission to be bold, to be strong.

How different life was for him, for his wife.

Wait—she was his *wife*.

No matter how short she planned for their marriage to be, the realization seemed to strike her all over again and had a shiver passing over her spine.

Once they were on the dock, men and wenches alike called out to them. There had to be nearly a hundred people there to greet them on the beach. There were more pirates in plaids, some in breeches, women in extremely low-cut gowns and a few children ran around several bonfires that rose high up into the sky. Hounds, too, wagged their tails and barked for their masters who'd returned. A mug of ale was shoved into the hands of each man that disembarked from a steady line of people passing the beverages from a barrel.

Beyond the beach was a massive twenty-foot-high stone wall, and from what she could see from inside the opened gates, dozens and dozens of buildings with smoke puffing out of chimneys surrounded a massive stone keep.

The Devils of the Deep truly had their own world. A well-fortified world. The sun shone down on them, bright and cheery, which seemed in strict contrast to the nature of their wealth.

Shaw took her hand and raised it into the air. "My wife, Lady Jane!"

That was all he needed to say, as his fierce expression said the rest. She was his. And anyone who dared to touch her or go against them had best be prepared to feed the fishes. It only took a breath before the entire crowd raised their mugs in the air and shouted their congratulations to their prince.

Three men pushed their way to the front of the crowd, and beside her, Shaw stiffened, standing taller.

The newcomers were huge. Full of muscle and bravado

and with a fearsome look about them that made her shudder. They wore plaids of similar coloring to Shaw, the same billowing black linen shirts and weapons gleaming all over their bodies. One stood out in particular as incredibly terrifying. A shock of blond hair covered his head, and piercing blue eyes seemed to cut her right down the middle. But most distinctive of all was a massive scar that ran from an eyebrow down one cheek, as though someone had hacked at his face. Oddly, it did not detract from the beauty of his features. He stood between the other two. All of them had their arms crossed over their chests, glowering in her direction. The man on his left was just as dark as Shaw and could be a younger brother. The third man had ginger-colored hair knotted on top of his head.

By the rood, she would not want to encounter any of them in a darkened alley or on the rough seas.

"Allow me to introduce my wife to ye, lads," Shaw said, tugging her forward, even though she resisted. They were just as terrifying as Shaw was. "Lady Jane." He pointed to his men. "These are my captains, my brothers in arms. Thor, captain of *The Sea Devil*." The man with the scar bowed his head. "Kelly O'Murphy, captain of *The Dark Sidhe*,"—he indicated the ginger and then pointed to the dark one—"Lachlan MacBeth, captain of *The Monster of Loch Ness*." The men bowed their heads to her, hands over their hearts.

Though the gesture was one of loyalty, it did not ease her fear when she looked at them. If Shaw wasn't there, how was she to know they wouldn't toss her out to sea?

"We grew up together, each of us adopted by the pirate king."

These were Shaw's brothers. All of them raised by a pirate king. How fascinating. And terrifying. Perhaps if they truly did consider themselves brothers, they would be more inclined not to kill her?

"And where is your pirate king?"

Shaw turned his regard back to the three menacing pirates. "They will protect ye with their life, Jane."

Jane suppressed a smile, feeling her hand tremble in Shaw's grasp. He gave her a fierce nod, no calming smiles like he had for her in the privacy of their cabin.

"Gather inside brethren," he bellowed. "We've a new adventure that awaits us."

With her hand still held in his, Shaw led her across a cobbled bailey and into the towering, stone keep. The inside was elegantly appointed and expensive beeswax candles dripped from chandeliers and candelabras. She wasn't sure why she was surprised, given his cabin was also well done up. Shaw MacDougall was a wealthy pirate and seemed to appreciate the finer things in life. That part of him was oddly endearing. When she was a lass, she'd often imagined pirates living in dark, dank hovels that resembled dungeons. Shaw lived like a king.

"The men will be gathered soon, and we shall feast." He led her up a circular stone stair and into a chamber designed for a woman. A rose and gold-colored tapestried carpet of woven flowers and angels matched the curtain on the ornately carved four-poster bed and the curtains by the window.

"This will be your chamber."

"We are not to share one?" The question was out before she had a chance to pull it back. It was not unusual for lords and ladies to have separate chambers. She'd just thought with him being a pirate…that perhaps he was not as civilized.

"Did ye share one with Douglas?"

"Nay, but—" She stopped herself before she told him exactly why she'd never shared one with her previous husband, and not because they were noble—but because they were not lovers. Well, she wasn't going to be Shaw's lover, either, but she'd assumed that was only known to her. Was it possible that he...? She shook her head refusing to read more into it.

He was a pirate.

Anything he did would likely not make sense to her.

"This is your chamber. A place ye can seek refuge, dress, and whatever else it is that ladies do. I did not say this was where ye'd sleep."

And there it was.

"Where shall I sleep?"

He jerked his head toward a wide oak door. "There. Come."

She didn't so much as follow him but was tugged along. He opened the door leading to an equally impressive and overly masculine bedchamber. Fit for a prince, and as lush as any pirate might love. There were massive wooden furnishings, fur coverlets, velvet, silks. Leather lined benches and chairs.

"Your chamber." She knew but needed confirmation.

"Aye." His eyes glittered on the bed, and when he turned back to her, they had darkened with passion.

Jane backed toward her chamber and watched a slow grin curl on his lips. "We will sleep here tonight, before we leave in the morning to find your Alexander."

"He is not *my* Alexander."

Shaw reached for her, stroking the side of her face with the backs of his fingers. "Aye, ye are no man's but mine."

She nodded, a warmth growing in the pit of her belly at the possession he had over her. That same spark of yearning that he'd ignited on the beach in Iona.

"Tell me, love, where are we going?"

For a moment, she'd forgotten what they were talking about. It was hard to regain her wits given he was stroking her skin so softly and making her think of kissing, making her think of being pressed deep into the thick mattress.

Somehow finding her tongue, she said, "He is in England."

Shaw jerked backward, a fierce frown darkening his face. "What?"

"The last place Livingstone could find him." She gave an apologetic smile.

Her pirate groaned. "Hell itself."

Jane shrugged with a little laugh. "If ye think it so, then aye."

"Where in England?" Shaw sauntered to a sideboard and poured her a glass of wine.

She accepted the goblet, their fingers brushing and sending a fresh frisson up her arm and through her chest, making her nipples harden. *Saints!* Could she not touch him without having such a visceral reaction? "London."

"Bloody hell." Shaw drained his own glass in one long swallow. "How are we supposed to get him there?"

Jane shrugged. This part of her plan, she'd not yet contemplated. "Ye're a pirate. Can ye not figure it out?"

He bared his teeth in irritation and poured another round.

"Perhaps I could send for him?" she offered.

Shaw stroked his chin with his thumb and forefinger as he thought over that suggestion. "Aye, that could work."

"All right, I shall do it."

"We will set sail and deliver the message when we arrive." He ran his hands through his hair. "My men will not like it. We'll have to make an arrangement with Poseidon's Legion."

"Who are they?"

"The English brethren. We've ties to them. If we dinna make an arrangement, they'll attack us when we enter their waters."

"Their waters? Are ye not all pirates? Can ye not enter

any water ye please? Is that not the nature of your business?" She'd not realized there were so many rules about being a pirate.

Shaw chuckled. "If only, lass. We may be pirates, but we've a code."

"What will ye offer them?"

Shaw shook his head. "Gold. Dammit, nay. That willna be good enough. Trésor Cove. 'Tis a pirate town north of Calais, a series of connected caves they've turned into a world of their own. The captain of Poseidon's Legion wants control of it, and I've been putting off helping him in gaining it."

"I'm sorry." Jane wrung her hands, realizing he was having to give up much in order to help her.

Shaw shook his head. "Dinna worry over it, lass. 'Tis how alliances are made. Besides, the alliance I made with Constantine was in hopes that we'd someday control the majority of the ports in Europe."

"How many ports are there?"

"Several in every country."

"Oh." An unimaginable number.

"Come on. Let us go below stairs. The men will be arriving."

In the great hall, as Shaw had expected, the room was filled with pirates reveling in the return of their brethren, and all curious about the woman their prince had taken as a wife. It was rare for a pirate to wed, let alone a prince. Having a family was dangerous. Made a man weak.

"Our Savage Prince has returned," shouted Jack. All in the room went down on their knee.

Shaw ordered the men to take a seat, and it was then she noticed how the great hall was set up. Instead of separate tables, there were many long far-reaching tables connected to form a circle around a centered raised dais with a massive round table. There were strategically placed breaks in the outer tables to allow entry into the center, where Shaw led her now.

It was amazing the way it was set up. So inclusive, rather than the prince looking down on everyone.

"We've a new treasure to unearth," Shaw called out to his men. "One that will change the tides of all our fortunes."

The men slammed their fists on the table in excitement.

"On the morrow, we set sail for England."

The slamming stopped, and the men gaped at him as though he'd grown a second head. "My wife, your mistress, has given to us the greatest treasure in all of Scotland. We just have to go to England to get it."

"And meet with Poseidon's Legion," Thor called out.

"Aye."

"What will ye give them in return for allowing ye safe passage?" Kelly asked.

"The French port."

The men grumbled at that, for they hated working with the English, but they also hated the brutal French pirates more. Shaw grinned. "I didna say we had to let Poseidon's Legion keep the French port for infinity, lads. Once we've gotten our treasure from England, we can set sail for Trésor Cove and give them a run for their gold coin."

The men all shouted their agreement, and then the room erupted with glee as Kelly leapt from his spot and began to dance a jig on the table. Lachlan tossed daggers at Kelly's feet, and she flinched each time the pointed end sunk into the wood. Thor looked on with a stoicism she found eerie, and beside her, Shaw looked on with pride.

Jane couldn't help but smile at the gathering of men and women, the jubilation, the sheer merriment. The pirate life certainly was different from that at court.

Beneath the table, Shaw squeezed her leg, and when she glanced at him, his pride was directed at her.

CHAPTER SEVEN

*A*s the men feasted and drank, sang and danced, the hours ticked by quickly. Jane was a silent observer, smiling, taking it all in. She'd even stood up to dance with him. Shaw watched his wife's eyes droop beside him. And then they'd closed altogether.

He waited for her to wake up, to startle when Thor pulled out his pipes and began to play, but if anything, she fell into a deeper slumber. In fact, he'd never seen anyone sleep so well in his life. Often, he'd heard the phrase slept like a bairn, but he'd not been around any bairns to know what that meant. But he would assume from now on that this was exactly what it meant. And the thought made him smile. Sweet Jane with a sensual kiss.

So he carried her upstairs to his chamber and laid her on the bed. Blond locks lay flat out on the pillow, creamy skin glowing in the hearth light. Triton's trident, she was beautiful. Delicate, and yet he knew just how strong she had to be to have gone through what she had. A surge of protectiveness crowded in his chest. Stroking his fingers across her forehead, he moved the hair away from her face and bent down to brush his lips in the same spot. She still smelled delicious.

As much as he wanted her, he wasn't going to wake her tonight. He wanted her fully awake when he took her for the first time. But that didn't mean they couldn't sleep together, which meant he had to undress her. He might be a pirate, but he didn't sully his bed linens with shoes or the clothes he'd worn that day.

Shaw lifted the hem of her gown to find her boots. Their soles were still covered in a dusting of sand. He unlaced them and slid them off, keeping an eye on her. She let out a sigh but did not stir otherwise. He unrolled her hose next, gritting his teeth as he touched the silky length of her long, curvy legs. Next, he managed to remove her gown. The threadbare, thin-as-air chemise had seen better days. Anger suddenly pierced through his fog of desire. A woman like her shouldn't have to wear undergarments that were obviously in bad condition. He wanted to rip the offending fabric off her body. But he stopped at the laces of her chemise. While he slept in the nude, she likely did not. Well, not yet. His wife would definitely sleep in the nude soon, though. Besides that, she would likely give him hell for taking *all* of her clothes off.

With a grin, he tucked her under the blankets, still amazed that all through his ministrations, she'd not moved.

Hours later, the moon high and dawn still some time away, he lay there in bed, stiff as a board, and unable to sleep at all. Arms tucked up beneath his head, he stared at the canopy, nostrils flared, tormented by her sweet feminine scent. Every soft sigh and whisper of movement on the sheets made him groan.

And just when he thought the agony couldn't get any worse, his tempting wife curled up on her side, her chemise riding up over her thighs and her hips, which wouldn't be a problem, except that her naked arse was now pressed up to his hip, branding him. If he dared to roll onto his side to face her, that raging part of himself would be pressed to the very heat of her.

Shaw ground his teeth, working hard to count the threads in the canopy overhead—a near impossible feat given the limited light.

Just the thought of touching her, of feeling her glistening warmth on his skin, had lust coursing through him at a rapid pace.

Shaw wanted her. Wanted her with a desperation he'd felt for no woman, with an intensity that threatened to make him go mad, to make him forget everything, including his duties, his code.

Feelings like that were not good for a man. And they were dangerous for a pirate.

His life was constantly on the line. His men's lives were constantly on the line. And now *her* life would be more on the line than it had been already. Just by being linked to him, she now had every enemy that had ever passed a threat his way hanging over her. *Ballocks*. Livingstone was nothing compared to some of the blackguards he'd dealt with.

Even more dangerous was the fact that he couldn't seem to control himself when he was around her. Any attention paid to a woman beyond what pleasures she could give him in bed was a weakness. Left him vulnerable. Hadn't he been down this road before, starting as a lad with his own mother?

Aye, Jane was bad for him.

But he couldn't let her go, because he needed her to get to the treasure. Needed her…period.

This lust that he felt, he needed to slake it, be done with it and get her out of his mind, else he'd put his entire brethren in danger.

And what was more important—the safety of his entire

fleet, his randy clan of Highland pirates, or giving in to that small plea of hers to leave her be? She was his wife. He'd bound himself to her in front of his crew.

A wife's duty was to satisfy her husband.

Well, Shaw was in serious need of satisfying.

As if she could hear his thoughts, Jane wriggled her bottom closer to him, rubbing her feet against his calves.

Perhaps he was not the only one with desires that needed to be sated. It'd been five years since she'd been married, not that he thought her marriage to a boy would have left her satisfied in the least. But he could.

He rolled to his side, feeling the heat of her silky bottom slide over his turgid shaft. A shudder passed through him. Slipping his arm around her waist, he tugged her back. Her belly was soft, flat, and he could feel the silky undersides of her breasts pressed to the back of his hand. He let out a groan, and to his surprise, Jane answered with a lusty whimper, arching her back into him.

"Jane," he whispered into her ear as he pressed his rigid cock tight to her lush backside. "I want ye."

She let out a gasp, jerking her head back and hitting him hard in the chin, causing him to bite the tip of his tongue. Pain seared, and he had a moment of impaired vision.

"Blast!" he ground out, tasting metallic.

Jane flew from the bed, standing right in the stream of silver light from the narrow windows. She whirled around to glare down at him. Her blond locks waved wildly about her head, and if he hadn't been certain Medusa lay dead at the bottom of the sea, he might have been convinced his wife was the fiery monster herself.

"What are ye doing?" Her voice was full of surprise as she gaped down at her threadbare chemise. The silver glow of the moon shone through the fabric and gave him the perfect view of her curvy, alluring figure.

Propping his head up on his bent arm, he patted the mattress. "Making love to my wife."

"How dare ye undress me without my permission?" Jane wrapped her arms around herself, skin flushed.

"Ye were sleeping, lass."

"And ye thought to make love to a sleeping woman? Is that the way pirates are?" She shivered, no doubt chilled out of bed. He liked to keep the room cool, and thus had pulled back the coverings from all four windows.

Shaw chuckled, amused by her outrage. If he didn't know better, he'd say she was a virgin bride and no marriage to William had ever transpired. "Ye were not asleep when I touched ye. Ye moaned, arched against me. Ye *like* my touch."

She shook her head vehemently, those blond locks waving wildly. "I did no such thing."

Shaw leapt from the bed to advance on her, stalking. "I beg to differ."

"Are ye calling me a liar?" She swept her gaze over his naked body, fully exposed in the moonlight.

"Aye, ye're a liar, Jane. Ye want me. I can tell by the way ye kiss me. By the way ye press your arse up against me, even in your sleep."

"Ah-ha!" She uncrossed her arms to point at him, and he got a clear view of pink, taut nipples beneath the sheer fabric. "Ye see, I was asleep."

God, she was every man's dream. "Ye were asleep until ye were not."

She frowned, re-crossing her arms when she took note of his gaze. "Ye're trying to trick me."

"Trick ye? I just want to lie with ye. Ye're my wife."

Jane shook her head, biting her lip. "'Twas only a handfast."

"Good in the eyes of all."

"Ye're a pirate." She pouted.

He wanted to bite those lips, to take them between his teeth and suck. "And ye're a dead woman, lass."

She had no answer to that, but her lower lip trembled, and he thought she might be very close to tears. Well, that wouldn't do.

"Dinna cry, love. I'll keep ye safe."

"I never cry." She stared at the bed. "I also never sleep." She turned a frown back on him. "Did ye put a drought in my wine?"

Shaw raised a brow at that. "Ye think I'd resort to drugging my wife just so I can lie with her?" He shook his head. "Love, if there is one thing I'm not lacking in, its women willing to fill my bed."

Her eyes widened as though he'd just revealed some great idea. "So, why do ye not go lie with one them?"

"Because. I'm married to *ye.*"

She shrugged as though that made little difference. "Husbands are not always faithful to their wives. And pirates are notorious liars."

Shaw stalked closer. "I should be offended at all the accusations ye keep tossing my way, lass."

"I am not trying to offend. Merely stating facts."

"Calling me a liar and philanderer. What else do ye think of me?" He was only a couple feet away from her now, and her eyes kept darting from his face to the space between his hips that jutted toward her like a battering ram. Her furtive, curious glances only made him harder. God, he wanted her.

"Big. Ye're very big." She licked her lips, changing the subject. "Tall, I mean. And broad."

"We'll fit, if that's what ye're worried about." There was only a foot of space between them now. He stepped closer, half a foot, and then closed the distance, bringing his hands to her elbows, gently touching her as he gazed down into her blue eyes. "I know ye had a lad afore, lass, but let me show ye what its like to be with a man."

"A man…" She breathed out the words, barely audible, and a shudder passed through her. But it wasn't one of disgust, because her nipples had pebbled hard against him, and she was staring at his mouth.

"Aye." He leaned down and brushed his lips over hers.

Jane stiffened against him, arms rigid, mouth clamped closed. But that didn't stop him, and she wasn't saying nay just yet. He slid his mouth over hers, soft at first and then more firmly, running the backs of his fingers up and down her arms. With every breath, her rigidity softened until she was sinking into him and sighing, parting her lips.

Though he wanted to plunge his tongue deep inside her mouth, he waited, teasing her, until it was she who was first to slide the tip of her wet, velvet tongue over his lips.

Bloody hell, it was tantalizing torment, and it took every ounce of his willpower not to lift her up, find the nearest piece of furniture to leverage her against and swiftly plunge deep.

But the more she kissed him, the more he wanted. He ran his hand up over her ribs, cupping a breast at the same time as he clutched her bottom and lifted her enough to press his hard length against the apex of her thighs. She gasped into his mouth, clutched his arms, but she didn't push him away. A brush of his thumb over her nipple had them both groaning. Shaw slanted his mouth over hers and let her have it, claiming her in a heated, carnal kiss that told her all he wanted to do with her, just not in words.

Jane didn't pull back. She kissed him harder, learning swiftly what he liked, and better yet, what she liked. Her hands shifted from clutching his arms to up around his neck, and she brushed her breasts provocatively against his chest.

"We canna…" she murmured, rubbing herself on him. "We canna…"

"Whatever ye desire, love." Oh, devil take it, she was going to be the death of him. Had he just agreed to do as she asked? To *not* make love to her? Hell, she was crushing herself against him with wanton abandon. Did she even know what she wanted? He had to take her at her word. He'd vowed not to claim her fully until she begged.

Well, if he wasn't allowed to make love to her, he was going to damn well make her want him just as much as he wanted her.

Not wanting to frighten her but needing to touch her all the same, and knowing that taking her to the bed would scare her out of whatever desirous trance she'd fallen into, Shaw backed them toward a bench at the base of the bed and sat, pulling her down beside him and swiftly lifting her legs over his thighs. From there, he was able to glide his fingers up under her chemise, stroking behind her knees, the tops of her thighs, until she instinctively parted her legs.

Sweet heavens, he could feel the very heat of her radiating down those thighs, and it was a sweet torture to wait the seconds it took to reach her center.

He slid his fingers over her glistened folds, and when she stiffened, he crooned, "God, ye're beautiful," against her ear and bit her lobe. "I love the way ye feel."

Her stiffness retreated, and she clung to him, tilting her head to the side as he trailed his lips down her neck to her collarbones and then even lower to trace his tongue over her taut nipples.

Jane moaned as he teased her breasts with his lips and her slick folds with his fingers, finding the tight little nub that sent bundles of fiery pleasure rippling through her. She trembled in his arms, her breaths coming in pants. Bright blue eyes were wide, then heavy-lidded, then wide again as she fought against her own willpower.

No boy lord would have been able to give her what Shaw could. Perhaps if she knew the pleasure to be had in his bed, she would come to him more willingly.

"Let go, Jane," he murmured against her breast.

"I canna." She gasped. "I canna."

"Aye—" he dipped a finger inside her tight sheath as he continued to circle his thumb on her nub, "—ye can. Let go for me, love."

Thighs trembling, gasping for breath, she rocked her hips tentatively at first, and then judging by her cry of delight, she realized how good it felt to move against his hand, and her rhythm increased.

"This…is…wicked," she crooned.

"But it feels good, aye?" He captured her lips as she said agreed and kissed her deep.

Not more than a few breaths later, her body tightened around his fingers, and she let out a loud cry into his kiss, shuddering as a climax took hold of her. Shaw stroked her until the quaking subsided and she sighed and loosened her grip on his neck.

He was harder than granite, and if she so much as gave the word, he'd lift her up and plunge deep inside her.

"That was…" she started to say but trailed off, avoiding his gaze as a heady flush covered her skin. "I've never…"

Shaw grinned. Damn, that had been good. "I'm glad I could give ye pleasure, love."

She bit her lip, peeked up at him. "Shall I give *ye* pleasure?"

Mo chreach… His gut tightened. "Och, love, ye already have."

"Then ye have felt what I…felt?"

Shaw leaned forward and gently bit her lower lip. "Aye," he lied, for if he allowed her to touch him, to give him the release he so desperately wanted, he'd end up taking her rough and hard. Pirates may be known for plundering and pillaging, but Shaw was going to draw the line with his wife.

CHAPTER EIGHT

*J*ane woke with the dawn, feeling more rested than she had, well, ever.

She lay on her side facing the wall and the open windows, which brought the scent of the sea and a gentle breeze. Rolling over, she prepared to smile at her husband but found the bed beside her was empty. She patted the place where Shaw had lain. It wasn't cold. He must have woken not too long ago. When she slipped out from beneath the covers and stretched, she felt a renewed energy rush within her veins. And a chill. The room was so cold. She rubbed her arms, shivering. The floor was frigid enough to freeze her toes, and she hopped over to the rug to warm them a little. The bed hadn't been this cold. Shaw's heat did amazing things.

Amazing things…

Her eyes fell to the bench where he'd pleasured her. Heat washed up from her breasts to her face. Never in her wildest dreams had she ever have imagined… And likely, if she'd not called for him to come and help her, she wouldn't have felt…

any of the wonderful sensations that had rippled along her limbs.

His words came back to her, about lovemaking being a man's duty and not a lad's... An involuntary shiver passed through her. Oh, how right he was. After what they'd experienced, she couldn't imagine anyone else sliding their hands between her legs, or pressing their mouth to her breast.

She was surprised to still be a maiden this morning, surprised he'd listened to her plea and surprised she was even able to voice it, especially when he'd laid her out on his lap.

For there was an intense curiosity to call him back to his chamber so they could kiss some more.

Leisurely, she walked from his room through the door leading to her own chamber to find that laid across the rose-gold coverlet was a beautiful gown of sky blue and silver trim, a crisp linen chemise with silk ribbons, a new pair of soft wool hose and smooth kid-leather boots with silver buckles.

It had been so long since she had anything pretty to wear. Jane slid her fingers over the soft silk of the gown. This was too beautiful to wear on the ship. She'd ruin it. The saltwater spray would leave dimples and stains in the fabric.

"Do ye like it?" It was Shaw, standing behind her in the doorway, leaning on the frame, arms crossed over his chest.

Heaven help her, he was too handsome for his own good, and certainly too stunning for hers.

A blush crept over her as she stared at his arms and recalled the way they'd felt wrapped around her. "I love it. Thank ye."

A knowing grin curled his sensual lips. "Put it on. I want to see."

"All right." She waited for him to leave, but he didn't. Standing there like a fool, she gazed at him and then the clothes, unsure how to ask him to leave so she could change, and then felt all the more foolish when she recalled the way she'd let him touch her the night before. She supposed undressing and redressing in front of him would not take away from her virginity and was no less scandalous than what they'd shared when the sun was down.

Turning her back on him, she slipped her worn chemise over her head. A shiver coursed over her, more so at the way his gaze burned into her back than the sudden chilly air touching her naked skin. Her breath hitched, and she stood frozen for a moment before she was able to regain her senses. When she did, she was quick to put on the new crisp one, sighing at the feel of the fabric sliding over her skin. Nothing had ever felt so good against her—except maybe his hands. The fact that he'd picked out these garments for her, that he was watching her dress, made it seem as though he were the one slipping them over her figure. Traitorous nipples tightened, and she squeezed her thighs together. Dressing had never been so...*sensual*. A fleeting sense of disappointment floated over her when she pulled on the blue gown, tightening the laces in the front. Whatever this was, this teasing dance, it was almost over. But when she went to grab the hose, she found her fingers brushing over Shaw's.

"Allow me, lass." His voice was gravelly, as though he found it hard to speak.

"What?" Jane glanced at him, seeing the way his eyes had darkened with desire. How could she argue with that stare? But she did. "Nay. I can do it myself."

"I know ye can. But I *want* to."

The pirate prince knelt on the floor before her, and she all but melted. He waited, and she found herself nodding. Shaw lifted her foot onto his muscular thigh and then slipped her toes into the wool, rolling the hose up to above her knee, making her gasp at the feather-light touch of his fingers.

Who knew that the act of putting on hose could be so…intimate?

Everything with this man was so intensified.

He tied the ribbons holding the hose in place and moved to her other leg. By the time he was done, her breath was erratic, her heart pounding and all she could think about was asking him to kiss her. She cleared her throat instead, working hard to get ahold of herself.

"Thank ye."

"Ye look beautiful." He still knelt on the floor looking up at her, and she had the absurd notion that he was kneeling down before her like a vassal, worshipping at her feet.

And while she rather liked that, it also made her want to kiss him all the more. "Thank ye. Please get up."

He grinned, leaping to his feet with an agility that was surprising for a man so large. He towered over her, his dark wavy hair as silky looking as her gown. He'd shaved the stubble from his face, and when he smiled down at her, she could see a slight dimple in his cheek.

"I canna wear this on your ship." She slid her hands down the silky skirts. "'Twill be ruined."

Shaw clucked his tongue in disagreement. "I've a cloak for ye to wear on deck. Besides, no wife of mine will be dressed in rags."

"Oh, so many gifts. And I've nothing for ye." She looked away, feeling suddenly shy.

"Ye are gift enough."

Jane narrowed her eyes, flicked them back at him. Why was he being so…chivalrous?

"Come now. The crew awaits us. I've had a meal prepared and sent to our cabin aboard the ship." He pulled a cloak from where it hung in the wardrobe and held it out to her.

"Nay, wait. I canna begin to thank ye, Shaw. My debts are piling higher than I think I shall ever be able to repay."

"Ye've given me Scotland's greatest treasure, Jane. Stop thanking me." He appeared serious enough that she nodded, though she mentally prepared to help in any way she could.

Outside, the sun had yet to burn the morning mist away from the sea's surface. The crew lined the ship, waiting expectantly to greet their captain. Though Jane had been hopeful there would be another female aboard, her hopes did not come to fruition. Shaw explained that a female on board was bad luck, and that even as his wife, she would normally remain behind. However, because she was the key they needed to unlock the treasure box, she would be allowed on board this time.

All four ships were readied, their sails high and the men singing a song about hoisting the mizzen and other such things she didn't fully understand. Before she'd been on the *Savage of the Sea*, she'd never realized how complicated it appeared to sail a massive galley. It was actually quite impressive to watch the way the crew worked in unison, each one having their own specific duty that worked in tandem with the man before and after him.

Shaw led her into his richly appointed cabin, all too aware of the hand he pressed to the small of her back, and the oak door that now stood closed.

Jane turned in a slow circle, taking note of the vast wall of books that he'd kissed her against, and then the pianoforte, the harp, the large ornate table, the huge four-poster bed, the rich velvet curtains, gold-gilded paintings, thick and lavish tapestries. It was truly a cabin fit for a king—or prince.

She sat down at the table where he indicated. Served on gold-plated chargers were delicious looking honey-buns, slices of ham and quail's eggs.

When Shaw did not join her, and indeed there was no

place set for him, Jane furrowed her brow. "I am to eat alone?"

"I'm captain of the ship, love. I have to man the helm."

"Oh." She'd not thought of that and tried to hide her disappointment.

"Stay here. Dinna venture out on deck. A ship is a dangerous place for a lass. There's plenty to do in here to keep ye occupied."

"What if I want fresh air?"

He walked to the porthole, opened it up and pointed out. "Fresh air."

Jane tried not to frown. "Thank ye."

Shaw grunted, distracted or perhaps needing to get out of the cabin, away from her. Whenever they were together, the air itself seemed charged. Indeed, she was surprised he'd not tried to kiss her this morning.

"I'll return later this evening." His tone was gruff.

She tried not to notice. "How long until we reach England?"

"First we sail to Cornwall. Perran Castle, the stronghold of Constantine le Brecque."

"Who is he?"

"He is the leader of Poseidon's Legion."

Jane nodded. "I recall ye mentioning needing their permission to sail."

"We dinna need permission exactly," Shaw said with frown. "Rather, I dinna want to engage with them as it will take more time to do so than to simply sail on. And if I'm not mistaken, this business with Alexander and the Black Knight is of the utmost importance, and we'd best not wait."

"Aye. Livingstone has likely been hunting Alexander for years. And he must have spies in England. Someone is bound to give away their position soon. If they havena already."

"Exactly. As much as I love to kick the arses of *Sassenach* pirates, I dinna want to do so at the expense of my treasure."

"Completely understood."

He left her then. She enjoyed the lavish breakfast and then went to peruse the bookshelf for something to read, finding a copy of *Beowulf*. Flipping open to the first pages, she was immediately intrigued and went to sit on the cushioned chaise by the porthole, breathing in the sea air and reading to the gentle rock of the ship.

Whatever fears she'd had about being married to a pirate, or about even getting involved with a pirate, soon faded away.

~

No more than an hour into their journey, Shaw saw the sails of an approaching ship through his spyglass from the west. Despite how many times he'd changed their course, they continued following in their direction. He was certain of one thing—the approaching ship was following them.

With his four ships and le Brecque's two, Shaw could easily overtake whoever it was, but engaging out on the sea was not in his plan. He had a strict schedule to stick to. Suffering any losses would put them behind that schedule, and put his crew, his wife and their mission in jeopardy.

"Blast it," he muttered. "Sail ho!"

"Everything all right, Cap'n?" Jack asked.

"Signal Thor, Kelly and Lachlan that we've got rats at the stern."

"Aye, Cap'n."

"And haul wind, Jack, we'll not be stopped by a bunch of scallywags."

Jack called out orders to the men and signaled to their other ships. Soon they were hauling arse through the waters, and the white sails of those who followed grew smaller and smaller until they were out of sight.

For several hours, they continued to monitor their rear, and as the sun started to set, the sails reappeared on the horizon at their stern.

"Blimey," Shaw growled.

"They want something from ye, Cap'n," Jack muttered.

"Aye. And they willna be getting her."

"Ye know who it is?"

"Pretty damned sure. Livingstone."

Jack groaned. "Not that bastard again."

"Aye. He wants Lady Jane, and he wants me on the gibbet."

"For the foul up at Edinburgh Castle?"

"Aye." Shaw didn't go into more detail than that. Livingstone had a lot to be angry about. Shaw's having gone back on their deal. Shaw having saved Jane instead of murdering her—and now once more, he'd thwarted the blackguard's plans where Jane was concerned. Having married her, offering her his ultimate protection would have Livingstone no doubt seeing red. On top of that, Shaw suspected Livingstone knew that he was going after what the man wanted most.

The man's reputation was at stake, not to mention all his hard work at covering up the existence of a king that was not under his control.

The bastard was likely already looking deficient to his peers for having given the pirates back to Shaw's care, and now those who wanted Alexander dead and buried would be even more irritated that Livingstone had fouled up once more.

Perhaps it would be best to face the bastard now while they were at sea, while he had had twice the guns and crew. Send a message at least that he wasn't afraid.

"Avast, lads!" Shaw called out. "Turn it about. I'm in the mood for a fight."

Loud whoops went up among the crew as they leapt to change up the sails and signal to the other ships that they were turning around.

The wind blew in their favor, helping them close the distance in short order. Shaw sailed with his three ships behind him, heading straight in the direction of the two royal galleons without veering off path. Livingstone, seeing that Shaw was heading straight for them, turned his ships, separating—always a bad idea.

Shaw navigated his four ships right between them, moving to stand up on the rail at the bow searching out Livingstone. The man was spitting mad, standing at his helm, red in the face, hands fisted at his sides.

"Cannons ready," Shaw bellowed.

Livingstone shouted something unintelligible that was lost in the wind.

"What was that? Retreat or die!" Shaw grinned widely. "Guns forward!"

Oh, how he wanted to shout fire. To watch Livingstone's ships be completely obliterated. But the truth of it was that if he fired, Livingstone would also fire. And though they were outnumbered, they would still be able to do some damage to Shaw's ships, and possibly harm Jane. What he was doing, threatening to fire, was risky, because if Livingstone was in a risk-taking mood—which might be the first in his sad life— Shaw would have to accept the challenge.

But as he'd expected, Livingstone raised his hands in surrender, his face visibly paling.

Shaw's grin widened. Och, but that had been too easy. Livingstone wanted him to board his ship, probably so he could attempt to run Shaw through, or at least take the lives of the six crew members he'd let go five years ago.

"Another day, Livingstone, ye bastard!" Shaw growled. "Cease following us, else I blow your ships to a thousand pieces and see ye sink into oblivion."

"Ye have something of mine on your ship," Livingstone sputtered.

"On the contrary, I've nothing that belongs to ye."

"A woman. The nuns at Iona saw ye take her. Give her over, and our business shall be done."

"The only woman on this ship is my wife, and I guarantee ye'll never get your filthy hands on her. And if ye try, well, my cannons are primed for eating wood."

Livingstone blustered. "I know ye have her!"

Shaw just raised a brow, because clearly Livingstone didn't believe that Lady Jane could be his wife.

"Sail on, pirate scum, but I will come after ye."

Shaw gave a mock salute. "I shall count on it."

CHAPTER NINE

*U*ntil now, Jane had not realized just how terrified she was of Livingstone.

Aye, she'd known him to be a threat—but the threat had always been a far off danger. Now he was visible. His face was right there, screwed up in anger, visible from her tiny porthole.

When the ship had made a hard turn and then sailed through the sea as though Davy Jones himself was on their tail, she'd leapt up from the chaise where she'd been dozing after a full day of reading only to see the ships ahead.

Being on a pirate ship, she'd assumed they were about to board and pillage some poor merchant or however these men went about making their fortunes. But then she'd spotted the flag. The royal flag of Scotland, and beside it Livingstone's terrifying crest of a man holding a cudgel in one hand and a snake in the other. Oh, how fitting for a man like Livingstone. For he was a snake that would strike a person until their dying breath.

Her enemy's serpent like eyes slid over the hull, and

seeming to spot her face, he demanded Shaw release her to his care. *Nay! Nay!*

For a split second, she'd been certain Shaw was going to hand her over. Why would he save her so many times if only to just give her up? Perhaps Livingstone had offered him a great chest of gold. Pirates could be bought with such things. And there was no guarantee that any ransom would be forthcoming with Alexander's apprehension. A chest of gold right in front of him was a sure thing.

Heart hammering, she sank to the floor of the cabin, shaking. Below her, she could feel the vibrations of the cannons being rolled to their firing positions.

Through the open porthole, she could hear the shouts, though she could barely make out what they were saying. She only caught snippets of words here and there that made no sense.

As she sat cowering like a fool, something inside her snapped. She was tired of running, tired of hiding, tired of being a coward. This was no way to live, quaking pathetically on the floor.

For the last five years, she'd known she was meant for something greater than a virtual prisoner awaiting her death sentence, and she wasn't about to let Livingstone or her pirate husband make her decisions for her. Not anymore.

With renewed resolve, Jane stood. There had to be something in this hugely ornate cabin that she could use as a weapon. A pirate wouldn't be a pirate without a stash. She searched the room, opening up a cabinet painted with scenes of a battle and trimmed in gold. And she wasn't disappointed. Inside, was an arsenal of weapons that gleamed in their holders. Swords, daggers, axes, maces. She looked at a hand cannon, but having never used one before, she was fairly certain she would blow her own hand off at best and her face off at worst.

A sound outside her door had her startling. Was he coming already to drag her up on deck?

Oh, what a betrayer he was! No gentle warrior was he.

Jane's fingers brushed the hilt of a sword. But she wasn't a fool. She'd never be able to take out Shaw with a sword. Likely, she'd barely be able to keep him at bay. He'd knock it away as though she held a comb out to him. The man was made of steel and could disarm her before she registered he was in the room.

Outside the cabin door grew silent, and she resumed her frantic search for a weapon she could actually use. Then she spotted a crossbow and a neat stack of sharp arrows in a quiver beside it.

This she knew how to use. She'd practiced a few times with her older brother when she was a lass, before she'd married wee William and wished she could use it on him. Ironic that she was now prepared to use it on her second husband. But if Shaw so much as thought she would go with Livingstone, that he could betray her in this way, he had another think coming—an arrow to the heart specifically.

Jane loaded the crossbow, sat on the chair facing the door and waited. As soon as the handle lifted, she stood, cocked the lever into place and prepared to let the arrow fly.

Shaw opened the door, a fierce frown already on his face that darkened when he took in the sight of the crossbow. A shudder passed through her, and she sought out the same resolve that had her searching for a weapon to begin with. *Strength, girl*, she thought to herself.

"Are ye going to shoot me, wife?"

"That depends." Her voice shook, making her frown all the fiercer.

He shut the door, crossed his arms over his massive chest and leaned back against the door as though he had all day and not one care in the world. "On what?"

"What your plan is."

"My plan? It hasna changed."

"Then perhaps I am imaging things, but I do believe that was Livingstone just outside my porthole."

"Ah, aye, 'twas." Shaw's gaze roved up and down her body, a slow grin covering his face.

She didn't like that grin. It was arrogant and made her think he believed she was a fool. Well, she wasn't a fool. That was why she'd picked up the crossbow to begin with, to show him she wasn't going to just be given away. "And?" she urged, frowning fiercely and jabbing the crossbow into the air as if to drive her question home.

"Careful with that, a crossbow is not a toy."

"I know it's not a toy, ye jackanapes."

He grinned. "Ye're verra pretty when ye're angry, love."

Jane let out a frustrated growl and waved it again.

Keeping his eyes on hers, Shaw said, "When I was a lad, I thought I would die."

Jane narrowed her eyes on him. "What has that to do with the current situation?"

He ignored her. "My father, Chief MacDougall, was not a verra nice man."

"Shaw, I will *not* go with Livingstone. Ye canna make me."

"Our clan fell on hard times. And so he decided to try his hand at piracy."

"Did ye hear me? I will not go! I willna allow ye to go back on our agreement."

"Well, as ye can imagine, being a pirate isna something ye just decide to do." He waved his hand at the crossbow. "Much like going from being a lady to an assassin, I imagine."

"I will not hesitate to shoot ye if ye try to take me off this ship."

It appeared she'd developed a sudden muted affliction, for he did not register that she spoke at all.

"So my father ended up sailing his ship right into the path of the pirate king of the Devils of the Deep. Fool that he was, he thought he could take the pirate on with his skilled warriors, but ye see the thing about pirates is, they dinna fight fair. They fight to survive, no matter the cost." At that, he uncrossed his arms and pushed lazily off the door.

For a split second, she panicked that he was going to attempt to disarm her and she was going to have to shoot him, but instead, he sauntered toward the porthole window.

Jane followed him with the crossbow, keeping it aimed now on his back, which seemed much less honorable. Could she shoot him in the back? Nay. She was actually beginning to believe she wouldn't be able to shoot him in the chest, either. She wasn't a killer. And she owed a debt to this man. Besides, part of her was starting to doubt whether or not he was going to give her to Livingstone. Not to mention, she was overly curious about the story he was telling. But she couldn't let that curiosity distract her.

"I was on board that ship with me da. And when he saw me peeking from behind a pile of crates, he offered me up as chattel to the pirate. Sold me off in order to gain his own freedom. I was eleven. And I didna want to be sold off to be a feast for the Devils of the Deep. For they looked like devils, laughed like devils and killed like devils. I was certain they must eat children. I wrenched a sword from a dying man's hands and raised it against the pirate king."

"Why are ye telling me this, Shaw?"

Though his back was to her, he turned enough that she could view his profile, could see the nostalgic grin curling his lips.

"The king of pirates laughed at me. Bastard dropped his sword and laughed his arse off. The men of the crew did the same. So I ran at him, sword extended, and he just swatted the blade away, knocking me down with it. His crew tossed my father back onto his ship and set fire to it. I watched me da leap overboard into a skiff and row away. Never once did he call out for me or look back."

Jane felt a pang of sadness for the father who'd abandoned him without a backward glance. The father who'd sold his son in order to save his own arse.

"I didna let that stop me from fighting. From running. I leapt overboard. Fought a shark. Fought every damned bloke on that ship. For years."

A shark? Saints... He really was a god.

Shaw turned around to face her, the muscle in his jaw tight, his gaze raking over hers and settling on her eyes, locking her in place. Her hands trembled. The crossbow trembled. Her shoulders hurt from having held it so steady.

"That man became my true father. He taught me to have faith in myself, even when my own blood didna have faith in me. Even when I didna have faith in the world."

Jane lowered the crossbow, unhooked the lever. "I dinna understand."

"Have faith, Jane. Have I let ye down yet, lass?"

She shook her head.

"Since the day I met ye, I've been saving your arse, just like my pirate king did mine. And I've fought a hell of a lot bigger monsters than that blackguard."

Jane had the sudden urge to laugh and cry all at once. A jolt of energy rushed through her. She glanced down at the crossbow, suddenly needing to let it go. But Shaw was right there, taking it from her hand and returning it to the cabinet full of weapons.

He turned back to her, and she held her ground, knees no longer knocking together as she stared at him. This was a man who was used to hardship. A man who'd known little love except for in the oddest of places—from a pirate king who'd taken him under his wing.

"What was his name?" she asked.

"Who?"

"Your king."

"His name is MacAlpin. He lives still. Back at Castle Dheomhan."

"He was there?"

"Aye."

"Why did ye not introduce me to him?"

Shaw grimaced and whatever pain she saw reflected in his eyes quickly faded. "He is unwell."

"And that is why ye are now ruler of the ships?"

He laughed at that. "Ruler of the ships? Aye. That is why."

"He did not have any children of his own?"

A dark look passed over his features. "A pirate's life is not exactly conducive to family."

"Oh."

Shaw ran a hand through his hair. "He adopted many sons."

"And ye must have been his favorite."

"Mayhap." He grinned with pride. "Or 'haps I was just the best."

Jane smiled and sank back onto the bench beneath the window. "Thank ye for sharing that with me."

Shaw shrugged as if he'd not just told her a dark anecdote of his past. In fact, the very piece that made him into the man he was today.

"It may be safe to say, I've seen ye at your worst, lass, and perhaps ye needed to know that I, too, have been despondent in the past. But know that I'm not going to just toss ye to that monster."

"I'm sorry about your father." She wanted to hug him.

"And I'm sorry ye were ever entangled with Livingstone to begin with."

She shrugged, tucking her knees up beneath her skirts. "Seems the lot of a lass, does it nay?"

"Nay. Just because ye're a lass, doesna mean ye should expect or accept that your lot in life is to be abused by men like that."

Now it was her turn to shrug. "Alas, Shaw, lassies are told from the day they are born that is exactly what we should expect and accept."

"Not anymore."

She raised a brow. "Says who?"

"Me."

"Ye're going to suddenly change the world? Verra ambitious of ye." She teased.

Shaw grinned. "I am under no illusions that I can do that, love, but if I can change it for ye, and if enough bastards see it, mayhap they, too, will change the way they treat women."

Jane cocked her head, studying him. There seemed to be a lot more than met the eye with Shaw. Despite being a pirate, who were known for their philandering lives of debauchery, he held a deeper respect for women than most ordinary men.

And it would appear that his men did, too.

Aye, they had wenches at their stronghold, and he'd alluded to having plenty of lovers. But, all of the wenches seemed happy. Not abused or downtrodden.

Though he insisted on a specific code of good conduct with women amongst his men, she would have thought to see at least some of the men behaving in a less than chivalrous way. But there hadn't been even one. Not a single slip. That led her to believe that this was a running precedent with Shaw. That for a long time, he'd made sure his men treated women not only better than pirates, but better than other beings with a cock between his legs.

She blushed at the vulgar thought. It would seem that in the company of pirates for less than two days, she was already starting to think like one. Shaw was rubbing off on her. Or perhaps allowing her the freedom she'd never had before. The freedom to be vulgar if she wanted to. The freedom to explore who she was and what she wanted.

And for some reason, that made her smile all the more.

CHAPTER TEN

*H*e'd told her too much.

Shaw knew that the moment he stared at her and felt a kindred spirit. The moment she passed him a secret smile that knocked against a deep part of himself he'd kept locked away for longer than he could remember.

Because of that, he quickly left her, backing out of their room without a word. He raced up on deck and set about working his men harder than usual if only to work off his own steam. Sweat soaked through his shirt, drenched his hair. And still he worked harder, sweating out the thoughts of her, the affects of her. And still her beautiful face flashed before his eyes. The way her mouth had opened when she moaned with pleasure. The way she'd smiled up at him as though they shared a secret. Like hell he was going to sleep in his cabin, for sleep was the last thing on his mind.

Rather than subject his resolve to further damage, Shaw slept on deck, definitely not preferring the chilly sea air to the warm sweet body in his cabin, but needing distance from her and the strange sensations she was tugging from inside his chest.

By the next afternoon, the long stretch of beach on the Cornwall coast came into view, and with it, Holywell Tower and Perran Castle—Poseidon's Legion stronghold. Perran Castle jutted into the sky just off the beach of Perranporth. Farther to the north, Holywell towered like the earthly Mount Olympus.

It'd been at least a year since he'd seen Constantine le Brecque, though they'd known each other for many years, just as they were both coming in their own. Their first encounter had been quite volatile when Shaw attacked the merchant ship Constantine was sailing with his adoptive father. Shaw had let the two of them go. The first time, he'd been merciful, but damn if Constantine didn't hold the attack over his head. Probably why their second encounter had come about. Constantine had attacked the *Savage of the Sea* to get revenge after wrongly assuming Shaw had seduced a devious wench away from him. Poor bastard hadn't perceived that wench's wiliness until Shaw pointed it out, and then Constantine had tried to rip Shaw's head off with renewed effort.

When Shaw had knocked away his weapon and offered mercy for a second time, Constantine had begrudgingly backed off. On and off, they'd been at odds with each other, but the bond had never been broken. If anything, it had been strengthened.

When death was on the line, Shaw knew he could always call on Constantine, and the pirate would be there for him. Sometimes Shaw had to pay, and sometimes he demanded payment for a favor.

Constantine had been attempting to negotiate with Shaw for the last year about gaining access to the French port. Shaw was going to help the Sassenach take it. Beat those French bastards —*les Porteurs d'Eau*, the Water Bearers, and their vicious captain, Nicolas Van Rompay, a man ruthless and evil to the core. Below decks, they made their victims row their ships with a pirate lashing their backs as they went. Shaw knew this because three of his men had been captured during a fight, and he'd had to enlist Constantine's help to gain them back. But the poor bastards had died from their injuries anyway. In addition to working their victims to death, the Water Bearers also chopped off their feet, so if they did by some miracle manage to escape the heavy chains that kept them at the oars, they couldn't run, and the blood and puss from their wounds just brought sharks to feed.

Together, Constantine and Shaw had executed the row boss, but they'd not been able to overtake the French who were bent on utter destruction rather than what most other pirates wanted—riches, treasure, freedom and wenches. The French fed on the blood of their victims. Unholy blackguards. Not that Shaw was a holy man himself, but he believed that the devil was true, and he believed in the sea gods.

During a siege, Constantine's quartermaster had been taken, strapped to the bow of Van Rompay's ship and left to die in torment. And Constantine wanted revenge.

As they approached, Shaw called for his flag to be raised so whoever was in the guard tower at Perran would know who he was.

Despite that, a loud boom echoed on the wind as the castle sent a cannon ball careening toward their ship. As predicted, it landed about a dozen feet from the starboard side. Just as it always did.

"Bastard," Shaw muttered. "Drop the skiff."

As he rowed toward shore, three more cannons were fired, all missing Shaw and his ship, but rankling nonetheless.

Shaw vacated the skiff in the shallow pools of the shore

and trudged up the wet beach with Thor, Kelly and Lachlan at his side.

"Ho, there!" called one of the men from the guard tower.

"Bugger off," Shaw shouted. "Get le Brecque. We've come to parley."

The pirate guard waved a crude gesture their way and then ducked out of sight. A moment later, the gate rose, allowing them entry into the castle bailey.

With their hands on their sword hilts, Shaw stared down the English pirate knights who lined the inside of the bailey. Covered in armor, their eyes glittered from inside their helms. Shaw shook his head. No matter how many times they'd seen him, fought with him, they still acted like he might draw his sword in their bailey. For most pirates, stabbing their allies in the back wasn't unusual. But he had a soft spot for Constantine. Maybe because the man reminded him so much of himself. Another brother in arms, if not by blood.

After a quarter hour, Constantine finally made his appearance. Tall and broad, Constantine was blond as a golden god with eyes to match. The men often teased that he was borne of the waves and lifted up to the sea gods as an offering. Likely they were jealous that no wench could look at Constantine without falling madly in love. Where Shaw was dark, Constantine was light. Exact opposites.

"To what do we owe the pleasure of Savage gracing our doorstep?" Constantine asked, a wide grin on his mouth as they approached each other in greeting.

"'Haps we've come to plunder your women and ravage your gold," Shaw jested, slapping Constantine on the back.

Constantine laughed and gave Shaw an equally rough punch to the shoulder. "You always were one for jesting, weren't you?"

Shaw frowned. "Bastard."

That only made Constantine laugh harder, but then he abruptly stopped. "Come inside."

Shaw glanced to his men and nodded for them to follow. Inside, the castle was dimly lit. Wenches lounged with men while servants refilled their cups.

"We were just finishing the nooning. Are you in need of sustenance?"

"Aye," Shaw said.

They took seats at the table and were served trenchers of roasted meat, bread and mugs of ale. Constantine eyed him up and down before finally saying, "Tell me why you've come."

"We need to cross the channel freely."

Constantine sat back and crossed his arms over his chest. "So you're wanting a letter of marque?"

"Aye."

"And what will you offer as a toll payment to cross without being boarded?"

Shaw rolled his eyes. He was only here out of respect for Constantine's claim on the channel. If he wanted to cross without permission, he damned well would. "The French."

Constantine raised a brow. "The French?"

"Aye. Trésor Cove will be yours."

"Why are you crossing the channel?"

"My wife." Shaw didn't expand.

"My arse." He slammed his hand on the table with an obnoxious laugh. "Why are you crossing the channel?"

Shaw raised a brow in challenge. "I just told ye. My wife."

Constantine narrowed his eyes, as if deciding that maybe Shaw wasn't lying. "You have a wife?"

"Aye."

"I want to meet your woman."

"Not bloody likely."

"Where is she? You wouldn't have left her back at Scarba. She's on your ship, isn't she?"

Shaw glowered, annoyed that Constantine had guessed that. "If she's important enough to get you to help me with the French, which I've been trying to get you to do for the past year, you would never let her out of your sight. I want to meet her before I agree."

"Nay."

"Then we are at an impasse, and I reserve the right to raise my sword against you for having trespassed onto my territory."

"And ye can rest assured that I will not rest in seeing that Trésor Cove is never in English hands."

Constantine chuckled and stuffed a piece of chicken into his mouth. "Interesting terms we have here. How about we battle for it?"

"Battle for what?"

"Whether or not I see your wife."

"Bloody hell, Constantine. Ye know it wasna me who was rutting your lady."

"She was most definitely not a lady."

"Needless to say. 'Twasna me."

Constantine eyed him. "All right. You'll have the letters of marque, but we'll accompany you."

"Nay."

"Why not?"

"We'll come back here when our business in England is done."

"You still haven't told me what your business is."

"Nay, I havena." Shaw stabbed his meat.

"What is the big secret?"

Ballocks, he wasn't about to tell him the truth. "My wife's family is in need of rescuing."

"You married an English lass?" Constantine looked skeptical.

"Extended family."

"Hmm… We'll still come with you."

Shaw gritted his teeth. "Nay."

"That is the deal, Savage. Either I come with you, or you let me have a night with your wife."

Shaw slammed his fists down on the table. "*That* is never going to happen."

Constantine raised his mug of ale and smiled. "Looking forward to traveling with you. It's been a long time."

～

IT WAS A LOT EASIER TO COME OUT OF THE CABIN AND WALK the deck now that Shaw wasn't on board. While two of the sailors tried to warn her against it, one glower down her nose as though she were their nursemaid had them nodding solemnly and ducking their heads before they went back to their duties.

Jane walked to the rail, gingerly stepping over coiled rigging and ducking out of the way of the men as they worked. She wouldn't put it past Jack to haul her back to the cabin like a sack of potatoes if she proved to be in the way. A swift gust of wind whipped her hair as she viewed the beach and massive castle towering over it. Four skiffs had been pulled up onto the sand. But Shaw and his men were nowhere in sight now. They'd gone into the eerie-looking castle that flew a flag she'd never seen before—one with a dragon on it.

"My lady, have ye had enough of the sun yet? Ye should be gettin' back into the cabin, else Cap'n Savage will be having my arse skinned on the gibbet." Beside her stood the rat-faced Jack. He was at eye level with her, muscles bulging out of his shirt, ready to pop the linen at its seams.

She sniffed at him. "I dinna think your captain would do such a thing to ye. He counts on ye."

Jack laughed hoarsely and tugged at his collar. "Then ye dinna know him well."

Jane just smiled, believing she probably knew him best out of everyone. Shaw seemed to let his guard down when he was with her, even while he was ruthless to everyone else.

"Please, my lady, I'll bring ye something sweet, like a honey cake or some such."

"Are ye bribing me, Jack?"

"Well, 'tis better than tossing ye over me shoulder, as I'm sure ye'd agree. Besides, Cap'n wouldna like that."

Jane sighed. "Nay, I suppose he wouldna. And neither would I. I might have to skin ye on the gibbet myself."

Jack's eyes widened. "Pardon my sayin' so, my lady, but I think Cap'n Savage has chosen a fine lass for a lifelong companion."

"Hmm." Jane cocked her head to the side and narrowed her eyes, trying not to laugh. "I'm glad ye think so, Jack."

Jack looked sideways, unable to meet her gaze. "Well, then. A honey cake?"

"Nay. I dinna think I will oblige ye in that."

Jack mumbled something under his breath.

"And I'll be certain to let your captain know that ye did try most earnestly to keep me locked up, but I just wouldna remain. In fact, I'm happy to retrieve the crossbow and tell him I threatened to shoot ye."

Jack eyed her skeptically and then looked as though he might have a fit of apoplexy as he gazed over her shoulder.

Jane jerked her gaze back toward the shore in time to see her husband marching out of the castle with his men. Every time she saw him, he took her breath away. His dark hair blew in the gusts of wind coming off the sea, as did the plaid he wore around his hips. He and his men made a fearsome foursome, but she only had eyes for him. Without knowing him, she would say he certainly lived up to his Savage moniker, and to look upon him was to invite nightmares. The blades gleaming at his hips promised death by a thousand cuts, if one could be so lucky. And yet she knew he could bring pleasure with those hands, not just pain. Intense, heart-stopping pleasure.

"Too late," Jack muttered with a groan.

Though she couldn't see his face, she imagined her husband was staring right at her. His head was certainly turned in her direction, and the prickle she felt along her spine had to be his fierce glower. She'd directly disobeyed his order to remain in the cabin. What had possessed her? Perhaps it was the intense need for air, and not just the kind she could gain from the porthole. Mayhap it was that he'd been ignoring her for days, and so she sought to gain his attention even if it were negatively. Why had he been ignoring her?

She was miffed about it. Only having the company of the swabs who brought her meals and seemed too nervous to answer any of her questions.

At least she wasn't pointing a crossbow at him this time, so she supposed he wouldn't be so angry with her, would he? But that didn't seem to be the case. Shaw started shouting at her the moment he was on the water, pointing and bellowing like a man gone mad. She raised her eyebrows and watched as though she were studying an exotic creature, all while Jack pleaded for her to go back to the cabin before their captain returned.

But Jane remained, tempting fate, tempting his ire, wanting to irritate him as much as she'd been aggravated at being locked in a cabin for days like a tarnished prisoner unworthy of his company.

Though her heart lurched in her chest at the way he flew up the hemp ladder and sailed over the side of the ship, she held her ground. If she weren't certain he was a man, she might have thought he was a demon with supernatural powers.

His glower was intense, eyes bright with fury.

"How dare ye disobey me?" he growled, advancing on her.

The men of the ship backed up, perhaps afraid they were about to witness their captain flay his wife, but none of them were brave enough to stand up for her.

Jane opened her mouth to answer, but she was too shocked to say anything. Jack had the gall to nod emphatically as if to further prove the point that she'd disobeyed an order, and that he'd known that and tried to reason with her. The image might have made her laugh if she wasn't starting to get a few prickles of fear. Would he tie her to the gibbet? Had she tested his patience a might too much?

Holding her head high, she said, "I wanted fresh air."

"I told ye to remain in the cabin." He stabbed his finger toward the closed door that was to be her prison. "Never to come out. Ye directly went against my orders. Do ye know what happens to men when they go against my orders?"

She shook her head, feeling her belly flop. "Nay, but that is irrelevant as I am a woman." Oh, why was she goading him? His men gasped, taking another step back at her insolence.

Shaw's emerald eyes glistened with fury. "They get killed," he growled, picked her up, tossed her over his shoulder and stomped toward the stairs to their cabin.

He surged through the door and slammed it closed behind them. He tossed her onto the bed and came down on top of her, covering her completely with his large, muscular length.

Jane shoved at his shoulders, suddenly very afraid. "What are ye doing?" This was not the man she knew.

His eyes blazed with fury. The normal control he exhibited seemed to have deserted him, and with it, the man she knew.

Shaw gripped her hands, put them above her head on the pillow, pinning her legs with his until she was completely immobile.

"Ye are mine." He emphasized every word. And then his guard dropped, and behind that blazing fury, she witnessed something new. Something different. A maelstrom of emotion that threatened to eclipse them both as her heart reached out for his.

But as much as her heart hammered against his, Jane couldn't just back down. She wouldn't be bullied. So she narrowed her eyes. "For now."

"Nay." His low tone was menacing, but she ignored it.

"Aye. That is why we handfasted. Ye plan to be rid of me." Why did that sound like an accusation? And why did she sound hurt by it? Wasn't that what she wanted?

"I willna give ye over to that clod." He jerked his head toward the door, toward whoever it was that he imagined was coming for her.

"What clod?" She frowned, confused. "Livingstone?"

"Le Brecque. He is going to try to take ye from me."

Her insides warmed then. All the anger, the menacing tones, it wasn't because he was mad at her, it was because he was mad at himself, at the emotions that brewed inside him, threatening to do him harm. "Are ye jealous, Shaw?"

He scoffed. "I never get jealous."

She raised a challenging brow. "Then why have ye pinned me to the bed to tell me that ye willna be letting me go to some man I've never met? Ye wanted me to have faith in ye, have faith in me."

There was a flicker in his eyes, and even when he tried to shutter them, she could still see it. "What if I dinna want to be rid of ye?"

She didn't say anything, because she didn't believe him. He was a pirate. And also because she didn't know if she could stay with him. Sailing the seas, living lavishly and without the law all sounded well and good, but she'd only been with him for a couple days, and already they'd encountered enemies. Death was a very real possibility every second of every day.

Even still, she needed to appease him. "I promise, I will not leave ye for any clod."

"Any *man*," he stressed.

"Any man." Did she mean it? Was she serious? Saying those words at first had been a way to appease him, to calm him. But the moment they were out of her mouth, something different altogether warmed in the pit of her belly. Jane didn't want any other man. When she thought of her future, the only one who felt right, who had ever felt right for the past five years, if she were being honest, was him.

Shaw sighed as though she'd just given him the greatest gift and then bent to kiss her.

CHAPTER ELEVEN

*B*last it, but he wasn't fit for sainthood!

With a wife as beautiful and tantalizing as Jane, it was a surprise to Shaw how much restraint he'd been able to exhibit over the last two days.

But was it truly restraint, or something else?

Avoidance might be a more accurate term.

First, he'd avoided her by sleeping on the deck and ordering the swabs to see to her needs. Now he'd left her in the cabin once more to sleep on the deck all over again because he couldn't seem to control the storm raging inside himself. The way he'd felt when he saw her standing on the deck, so stunning, enticing, the jealousy—and, yes, he hated that jealousy was exactly what it was—that he'd felt when Constantine said he wanted to sleep with her, came back to him full force.

When he saw her standing on the deck of the ship, her golden locks blowing in the wind, he'd been struck with a number of emotions, besides jealousy, the strongest of which was the mind-blowing need to possess. To kill any man who dared threatened his possession. *Mine. Mine. Mine.*

Constantine, at once his ally and his adversary, had not let any alliance they might have ever get in the way of stealing a woman from him. In fact, he seemed to take great pride in tempting Shaw's lovers. There had been three now that he'd stolen right out from under Shaw. Likewise, Shaw had paid him back in kind.

But this was different.

Jane wasn't a mere wench, but his wife. And the woman he'd not been able to stop thinking about for five years. A lass who made his heart skip a beat, made his body rock hard the minute he laid his eyes on her.

Jane who came apart in his arms when he touched her and then begged him not to possess her fully.

He was still shocked that she'd promised not to leave him for any man.

Och, but any man, even fictional, made him crazy with jealousy.

Triton's trident... He wanted to possess her, but it would seem the possession had been entirely her doing.

Shaw raked his hands through his hair and then scrubbed them over his stubbled face. He'd barely slept with the tangle of deliberations running amuck in his head. He was quick to wake the crew and go about his day, though contemplations of Jane were never very far.

Blast it all, his life had been exceptional before she'd sent that missive. Before he'd seen her in Edinburgh.

Perfect.

Whisky, women and mayhem. The three things he loved the most.

Och, but if he were being honest, that was not the truth, for he'd enjoyed their brief sojourn five years before on the way to Iona. He'd been content with only exchanging letters with her, and disappointed when it was obvious to do so would only put her in danger.

And now he found himself having a conscience. Found himself wanting to go and see his wife. *Wife!* He was married, dammit. Hell and damnation, how had he let that happen? A pirate's life was not conducive to family. The more ties a man had, the more that could be taken away. On the daily, he was trying to save his own arse and that of his men, how was he supposed to factor a woman into that—and if she ever submitted to her desire for him and they made love, the child that could come from that?

The thought of a child was what kept him away from her these last two nights. He could imagine that child, looking much like himself, standing in the center of a burning ship deck as men fought to the death all around him and the wood turned to ash, the ship crumpling and sinking into the depths of oblivion. Swallowed whole by a kraken.

"Nay," Shaw growled. He could not have a child with Jane. Which meant he could never make love to her.

Which meant she'd been right when she'd said he wouldn't keep her.

Och, but that thought had a searing pain tearing through his chest. But this was for the best. For both of their safety.

"Cap'n?" Jack came up beside him. "Did ye say something?"

"Nay."

He needed to get his mind off his wife. Behind him sailed Constantine with one ship. Shaw had left his other three at Perran with Constantine's men, as all their ships sailing for London would have signaled to the Royal Navy that they were about to be invaded. Two merchant ships with separate sails and crews would not ring any alarm bells.

By the time the sun set, the *Savage of the Sea* would be traveling up the Thames River toward London to deliver the message to the Black Knight and Jane's uncle. Constantine would remain in port with the Savage until they returned with Alexander and his guardians. Shaw had yet to tell his ally just whom they were retrieving, and he didn't plan on it, as Constantine would most assuredly want in on the take, and the last thing Shaw needed was another battle on his hands.

Already, Livingstone would be tailing them. Even though Shaw had threatened to kill him, he knew that wasn't enough to stop the blackguard, but sailing into English waters just might.

Hell, disembarking in England was going to be tricky for Shaw. Or maybe he'd get lucky enough since the country was in its own state of turmoil between the House of Plantagenet and the House of Valois over who the succession of the French throne would go to that they wouldn't even notice them. That damned war had been going on for a hundred years at least. From what Shaw had heard, negotiations between England and France were going nowhere, save for yet another bloody battle. Hell, as a Scot, he knew just how damned stubborn the English were when they wanted an entire country to bend the knee.

Perhaps a Scot wouldn't be noticed given the county's current concentration, though he didn't doubt it was going to be risky infiltrating London. The thought of Jane in danger sent his heart into palpitations, but there was no other way. After careful deliberations with Constantine, Shaw had determined the best way to get the message to Jane's uncle was to go himself, and the best way to get the man to listen was to bring Jane with him.

"'Tis time to change the flags," Shaw told Jack. "For the next few days, we are merchants."

"And what will we be trading, Cap'n?"

Shaw smiled. "Salt." Constantine had let him borrow crates upon crates of salt, though the bottoms of the containers had been filled with bags of sand. Aboard his own ship, he had pepper they'd stolen together from the Spanish. It was worth a fortune.

"Aye, aye, Cap'n."

As they hoisted their vague flag, Constantine did the same.

They sailed into the Thames with no one caring what they were about. His men had cleaned themselves up, looking like a ragtag crew of swabs rather than pirates on the account. Those who'd been growing entire nests in their hair had their heads shaved. All beards were neatly trimmed. The lot of them were almost presentable.

Jane had done her hair up prettily and was wearing the blue silk gown he'd given her. She was a vision, and when they disembarked the ship, the dock master's eyes were more interested in Jane than they were in the faux manifesto Shaw had cooked up.

They walked along the port, rented two horses and then rode up the cobbled road in the direction the horse master had indicated.

The docks and surrounding neighborhoods in London stank of shite and smoke and decrepit souls. The perfect place for a pirate to find a new crew.

And also the perfect place to hide a king.

They found the house a mile or so away, and when they knocked, it was answered by an old woman who looked to have seen not only better days, but better decades. Gray hair was knotted at the top of her head, and she hunched beneath a threadbare shall, the bones of her shoulders jutting visibly beneath the fabric.

"What do you want?" she barked through several missing teeth and loose lips.

"I'm here to see my uncle." Jane's Scottish burr was still evident, though she'd tamed it down, sounding almost like it was in her distant past.

"Who's that?" the old woman croaked.

Jane straightened, not allowing the woman's grouchiness to intimidate her. "Edward Lindsay."

For a brief moment, Shaw was certain they'd been given the wrong address, but then a slim man appeared behind the old housekeeper.

"Thank ye, Helen, that will be all."

The old woman grumbled something, backing away. She passed Shaw a look that said she'd be watching him. He only raised a brow in her direction.

"Jane, what are you doing here?" Uncle Edward said but did not invite them in.

"Let us pass." Shaw stepped forward, until he saw that Edward held a pistol in his hands.

"'Tis loaded." His tone did not indicate a hint of emotion. He could have asked if they wanted a cup of ale for all it revealed. "Do not take another step."

"Uncle Edward, this is my husband, Shaw MacDougall."

Edward narrowed his eyes. "Why have ye come?"

"'Twould be best if we spoke inside." Jane's tone brooked no argument, and after a lengthy perusal of Shaw, Edward finally stepped back.

"I will not hesitate to shoot either of ye."

"I dinna blame ye," Shaw said.

Edward showed them into a darkened drawing room, which was stuffy and musty. The walls had been white-washed once, but they'd long since turned a dingy yellow, and black near the hearth. The air was thick, as though a window was never opened. "Sit. Wine?"

"Nay, thank ye," Jane said.

"Good, because I dinna have any. Only ale, and it tastes like piss."

"I'm sorry the last few months have been so awful for ye," Jane said.

"Better than dead."

"That is why we've come," Jane explained. "Livingstone came to Iona. He knows I was there. If he hasn't already questioned Father, he will do so soon, and then he'll figure out that ye exist."

"I see."

"He will be looking for ye, or he will have spies looking for ye. The Black Knight is known in parliament, someone will point them in your direction."

Edward nodded, still eyeing Shaw skeptically. "Then it was good of ye to come."

"Aye."

"Ye've a ship?" He directed his question at Shaw.

Leaning back in the chair, he said, "Aye."

"When did ye wed?" This time he asked Jane.

"Not too long ago. Shaw can be trusted."

Edward grunted. "That remains to be seen."

Shaw chose not to be offended by the man's distrust as he didn't trust Edward fully either. "'Twould be best if we left now, while 'tis dark."

"They are not here."

"What?" Jane asked, stiffening beside him.

Shaw did not react. He listened and waited to see if Edward would give anything away.

"Lorne took his sons out for entertainment."

"Entertainment?" Jane asked, unable to hide her incredulity.

"Aye." Edward did not appear to be disturbed in the least.

"What kind of entertainment?"

"A boxing match."

Shaw grimaced. By the casualness with which Edward was relaying the information, it sounded like this wasn't the first time they had done such things, which meant Lorne and Alexander were probably well known amongst the seedy types. Men who would sell their own children to make a few coins.

"Get them and meet us at the dock," Shaw said. "Ye'll know my ship by the wide red stripe down its center."

Edward nodded, surprising Shaw by not arguing. "We'll try to be there before dawn."

"Dinna try," Shaw warned. "We canna wait long."

Without waiting for Edward to react, Shaw ushered his wife from the house to find that one of their horses had been stolen. "Ballocks," Shaw growled. He glanced up and down the street and down a few alleyways to see if the horse had either run, or was still in the thieves care close by, but he returned with no results. *Bloody thieves!* And, aye, he was aware of how ironic that thought was.

"We'll ride back together," he grumbled.

He lifted her up onto the mount and swung up behind her. Och, but that was a torment of the worst kind. Her lush bottom pressed to his lap, warm and supple. Shaw gripped the reins, gritting his teeth against the desire coursing hotly through his veins and pooling in his cock. If only he'd not had to change out of his plaid for breeches, he might have still been wearing his sporran and been able to put a barrier between them.

But alas, inconspicuous garb had been paramount, and so now he had to deal with his breeches growing tight. Ballocks. His blood ran hotter than molten iron as they rode the mile back to the docks. It didn't help that his little wife squirmed and shifted every few minutes in the saddle.

"Sit still," he growled.

"There is something poking me."

For the love of all that was holy… He knew exactly what was poking her. If he wasn't so frustrated, he might have laughed, but instead he let out a low growl.

"Just sit still, we're almost there."

They returned the horse to the master and paid in full—perhaps a bit too much in full—for the one that had been stolen. The sly look in the man's eye had Shaw believing the horse master might have been the one to send the thief after them. He grabbed the man by the wrist and tugged him close. Before the man could blink, Shaw had a dagger at his throat.

"Are ye playing me, man?"

The horse master's eyes widened, and he shook his head violently. He stank of greed and fear.

"So, if I go into the back of your stables, I'm not going to find a horse fitting the exact description of the one stolen from me. The one I just paid ye a king's ransom for."

Again, the horse master shook his head so hard the skin on his face jiggled. "Nay, sir. But there are so many horses that look alike. How can I say you won't find one of them looking like the one you lost?"

Shaw growled, half a mind to take the man's arm off for thieving, but he didn't want to call any more attention to himself and Jane than he already had. Tonight, he was a merchant, not a pirate prince, and he had to remember that, else have the authorities coming down on him, and ruining his entire plan.

Beside him, Jane was silent, but he could feel her anxiety as though it were his own, so he left the merchant to his thieving ways and took her by the elbow, steering her back toward the ship.

"Do ye think he truly sent someone after us to steal the horse?" she asked.

"Aye. He saw your pretty dress, the cut of my cloak and thought to take us for a few extra coin."

"I am surprised."

"I'm not, lass. The dregs of humanity are most alive in port."

"Why in port?"

"Number of people coming and going. Goods that can be stolen, smuggled. Pirates, the like."

"I see. Do ye think Uncle Edward will have an easy time coming to the ship then with Lorne and Alexander?"

"Keep your voice down. There are a lot of listening ears around here, lass."

"I'm sorry."

"Dinna be sorry, just be careful. I think he'll figure it out. I'm more worried about the blokes Lorne has met at the betting fights. If he loses and canna repay, they will come after him."

"And then us."

"Aye."

A shiver passed through her, and Shaw tugged her closer. "I'll not let anything happen to ye, love."

"But how can I make sure nothing happens to *ye*?" She truly sounded worried, and it touched him in the deep cavern of his chest.

Shaw grinned. "Ye did say ye were good with a crossbow."

Jane giggled. "I didna say *good*. I just said I knew how to load it."

"Ah, then glad I am ye didna try to shoot me. Ye might have taken out your own foot."

CHAPTER TWELVE

*J*ane didn't let on how worried she truly was, for she didn't need Shaw to have yet another concern on his mind.

There was something strange in the way her uncle was acting, and she wasn't certain she could believe that Lorne, the Black Knight, would actually take Alexander to a boxing match. She wasn't as naïve as Shaw or her uncle might believe. She knew what went on at such establishments. London wasn't the only place where such seedy activities took place. There had been plenty in Edinburgh, too.

It was obvious Uncle Edward didn't trust Shaw, and perhaps, he didn't trust her either. For all they knew, Lorne and Alexander could have been hidden within the dilapidated domicile.

From outward appearances, in his smart cloak, fine breeches and clean-shaven face, Shaw MacDougall looked like he could be the well-to-do merchant he claimed to be. There was not a single hint of the brutal pirate life he led, except perhaps for the hardness in his eyes. The sharpness there gave way to the belief that violence was only a word or gesture away.

But all thoughts of her uncle's odd behavior vanished the moment they walked the length of the docks until they spotted their ship. A few torches had been lit, and from here she could see that the men were dancing, someone played the fiddle and laughter floated from the deck.

Shaw muttered an oath under his breath and stormed forward, dragging her with him.

When they reached the deck, one stomp of Shaw's boot and the revelry was silenced.

"Cap'n," Jack muttered, taking off his beaten cap and placing it over his heart, avoiding eye contact.

"What part of we must lay low was unclear?" Shaw growled, giving each of his men the eye.

Silence followed, no one wanting to take the blame or point a finger, and Jane was worried that Shaw might actually take a whip to them all. Finally, Jack stepped forward, the only one brave enough to face off with their captain.

"We was layin' low, Cap'n, but then if ye look about, a half-dozen other ships are all muckin' about and makin' a ruckus. We thought if we was the only serious lads in port, we would be bringin' more attention to ourselves than if we acted the part."

Jane glanced around, seeing that Jack was right. Many of the ships in port seemed to have men enjoying their evening. Laughter floated up from the various vessels, and music, too.

Shaw observed the other ships as well. Constantine and his men were also sitting on the rails and telling stories while passing a jug of spirits.

"Carry on, then. But if anyone takes too keen an interest in the ship, then ye'd best not be too deep in your cups to act the part."

"Aye-aye, Cap'n. We'll be sure not to." A wave of relief crashed over the ship.

Shaw nodded and turned to Jane. "I'll take ye to the cabin, lass."

Jane nodded, not wanting to irritate him further, even though she'd rather climb the mast and stake a claim there in order to see more clearly when her uncle finally arrived. He swiped a jug of something from one of the men, took a long draught and then, rather than take hold of her elbow as he'd been doing all evening, he placed his warm palm on the small of her back and guided her toward the stairs that led up to the captain's cabin.

Once inside, she took note of the cold supper of chicken, bread and carrots that had been laid out on their table, and her stomach rumbled in answer. She hadn't realized how hungry she was, and given they were so intent on arriving in port, she'd forgotten about supper altogether. A single beeswax candle in the candelabra burned giving off a faint scent of honey. Jane lifted the burning candle to light the others, illuminating the room better.

Shaw watched her with that same intense look he'd had on his face since the day before. Pinched and, if she were to hazard a guess, agitated. It was a wild turnabout from the passion and emotional intensity he'd exhibited. Jane didn't have a lot of experience with men, but she wasn't completely lacking in understanding. Shaw didn't like the feelings he had where she was concerned. Nay, he hadn't told her as much, but just by looking at him, she could figure it out. And even now, he looked like he wanted to run away from her.

"Please, sit. I'd hate to keep ye from your supper, lass."

Glancing at him from the corner of her eye as she made her way to the other side of the table, she said, "Will ye be joining me or returning to your men?"

Shaw started to back toward the door but then paused, glancing from her to the table. Finally, he shook his head.

Jane never begged for anything, but he'd been avoiding her lately, ever since telling her of his childhood, and she couldn't stand the idea of the growing distance between them, even if this wasn't a permanent situation. Locking her eyes on him, she risked asking, "Please, Shaw?"

From his expression, she might have asked if he would lick her boots. "All right, I will join ye, but only because ye begged." In a sudden change of mood, he winked when she pretended to bristle.

Good, they were teasing each other. That was certainly a better place than the tension that had filled the space between them over the last twenty-four hours.

"Ye're incorrigible, Shaw."

"As any proud pirate would be."

She thought he was more of a gentleman than a pirate, but she decided to keep that knowledge to herself. It wouldn't do to get him rankled if she wanted him to stay. Already she was treading in shallow water.

"Your uncle was lying," Shaw said casually as he slid into his chair.

"Oh?" she asked, not revealing that she too had found his behavior odd.

"Aye. Unless he's an extremely stupid man, but as ye are not an extremely stupid lass, I doubt that ye would put such a treasure in the hands of a man so easily able to lose it."

"Aye."

"So, tell me, what do ye think?"

Just what she'd been avoiding—any talk that might lead them down that tension-filled path again.

"I did find it odd that he would have allowed Lorne to take Alexander to a boxing match. The lad should have been locked up tight."

"And what do ye think they may have been doing instead?"

She shrugged. "They could have been there hiding, to be sure, and my uncle simply did not want to release those in his care to us, as he wasna certain if we could be trusted."

"I appreciate ye adding the we, but we both know it is me that he doesna trust."

Jane shook her head and bit into her chicken, chewing as she mulled her answer. "I am certain that he doesna trust ye, aye, and given that he doesna know ye and that he guards the greatest treasure in Scotland, one canna blame him for such. As for me, why should he completely trust me? I showed up unannounced and with a stranger demanding he simply hand the treasure over."

"I see your point. Do ye think he will come before dawn?" Shaw bit into a carrot, chewing slowly as he watched her, and she had the distinct impression she was being measured.

"I hope so. What will ye do if he doesna?" This answer she feared the most, because their agreement for her safety was based on her handing over the national treasure. And while they'd shared many passionate moments and he'd declared more than once that he wasn't letting her go, he'd also leapt backward and avoided her, as well.

She supposed she could make her way back to her uncle's house if she needed a safe haven, but who was to say that her uncle would accept her, or that he was still there? He could have packed up in a rush of panic and moved everyone out after their visit. There were no guarantees. He'd offered to protect the Black Knight and Alexander. He risked much already because of that.

"I willna turn ye out, lass."

Was she that easy to read?

"Ye're emotions read like an open book." He picked up a

hunk of meat and took a bite, watching her. "Even now, I can see just what ye're thinking."

"And what is that?" She tried to school her features into something plain, and when that didn't work, she scowled.

Shaw laughed. "Ye're thinking how irritating it is that I can see what ye think, that even when ye try, it's too hard to hide from me. Even that scowl ye have on your face is nothing but a ruse."

"Oh?"

"Ye're not mad at me."

"I assure ye, I am quite vexed."

"Not with me."

"Than with whom?"

"I'd say Livingstone for certain. And your uncle. Even though ye understand the reasons behind his actions, they still irritate ye. Ye want this business in London done with so ye can get back to your life."

Incredible. His read of her was pretty accurate. Except for the last part. "I have no life to get back to. I didna take vows at Iona, and given they all saw me leave with a pirate, and perhaps a few of them saw ye kissing me on the beach, I would certainly not be welcomed back into the fold of their saintly religious order."

A slow grin curled his lips. "Which is fine by ye, lass, because ye didna want to be a part of it anyway. Ye wrote it in your letters to me. And if ye were interested then instead of summoning me, ye would have taken vows and asked to be transferred to another abbey."

She pursed her lips, her gaze flicking to his lips as she recalled the kiss that had changed so much for her. Aye, she'd not known exactly what she wanted before. Even yesterday and this morning, she'd not known. And perhaps now, she was still uncertain, but the way he kissed her, the way she reacted to it, the way she liked talking to him, had practically begged him to sit with her to eat… The fact that her feelings were hurt when he avoided her, Jane knew that a life without love and desire, without Shaw, was not for her.

Aye, she wanted him. Wanted it all. But how could she make him see that was the right course to take? What if she was making a big mistake? What if it was only the danger she was in that made her want to align herself to the strongest man she knew?

"Ye want me to kiss ye." Shaw's gaze had darkened, his lids growing heavy with answering desire.

Jane scoffed and tore off a piece of her bread, shoving it into her mouth.

"Badly by the looks of it." He sat forward, pushing his food aside and leaning his elbows on the table.

She scoffed again and chewed harder.

Shaw chuckled and stood up, rounding the table at a slow predatory pace. "I'm happy to oblige, lass."

"Ye're wrong," she murmured.

He moved to the back of her chair, his hands on the wood as he bent to whisper, "Am I?"

"Aye." The word was barely audible above her racing heartbeat.

The backs of his fingers brushed her neck as he moved her hair back. "Then why is your pulse jumping?"

She was on the verge of retorting that she had no pulse, but that was just ridiculous, because one, of course she had a pulse and two, it was pounding so hard in her neck, she knew he could probably see it. Instead, she said, "Because I am nervous."

"About?"

She locked eyes with him. "Ye're such a good mind reader, why do ye not tell me yourself?"

"There are many things that make ye nervous, lass." He slipped her small hand into the grip of his large callused one and gently tugged her to stand. "Foremost on your mind was your uncle and the treasure. But that has changed."

Slowly, he turned her to face him, and her breath caught. The man was simply striking. She wanted to run her hands through his silky dark hair, trace the lines of his strong jaw and tug his lips with her teeth.

"Has it?" Her breath hitched as his hand slid around her waist to cup the small of her back, while her other hand remained a captive of his.

Gently, he swayed her, dancing to a tune that she couldn't hear, and then she realized that she could hear it faintly. It was the sound of the fiddlers playing on the deck just outside the porthole.

She allowed him to dance with her, following the lead of his steps, the gentle rocking of his body. If he'd asked her before, she would have said he didn't know how to dance. That pirates didn't dance. And clearly, she'd be wrong, for he danced better than any of the lords at court.

"Now ye're wondering where I learned to dance." He grinned. "And if I'll kiss ye."

"I was not," she admonished, realizing how much she actually did want him to kiss her, and that the thought had been placed into her mind without her even realizing it.

"I will, if ye wish it."

"I do not wish it."

"Then why do ye keep staring at my mouth?"

She jerked her gaze back up to his, not realizing that she had been staring at his lips. Wide, full and very kissable lips. Lips that had tantalized her before and made her want to explore them again.

"I was…reading your lips."

"Now ye're a lip reader? I had no idea ye had such a talent. What am I saying?" He mouthed something that looked very much like *liar*.

She frowned. "Ye're…such a pirate."

He laughed at that, his chest rumbling against hers. They were pressed so closely together she could smell the spicy, salty scent of him. He'd washed before they'd gone ashore, and all she wanted to do was bury her face against his neck or chest to breathe him in. Did he even have any idea of how intoxicating he was to her? And why, she had no idea. Perhaps this was natural, and if she'd not spent the last five years at an abbey, she might have taken note of such things, but then again, maybe it was just him.

"That I am, lass. And what does that make ye?"

"I dinna know," she whispered, her eyes falling to his lips once more.

He was right. She did want him to kiss her. Badly.

And she didn't have to ask. He lowered his mouth to hers, laying claim to her mind, body and soul. Life without Shaw would be infinitely different and she suspected disappointing. He was full of surprises and…desire. He made her body come alive with just a look, and the way he kissed her, so passionately as though she were the only thing that mattered in the entire world, made her melt.

She was going to miss him when they separated, which seemed inevitable as much as she was certain she didn't want to part from him. She wanted to be his wife. To sail the seas with him—though she didn't want to be a pirate herself, and she couldn't ask him to give that up for her. So she would do her best to be the best wife a pirate could ask for. Which was absurd. He'd hinted enough times that having a family was not in the cards.

Even still, if only to just take a piece of him with her, a private, passionate memory. Maybe holding onto her maidenhood wasn't as important as she thought. Maybe that was the memory she wanted to take with her. So, when he lifted her up against him, backing her toward the bench where he'd given her pleasure before, she didn't stop him.

Shaw laid her out like she was a fine treasure, and then he knelt on the floor beside the bench, kissing her, caressing her ribs, her hips. But nowhere else. And she wanted him, too. She squirmed and wriggled, shifting closer, until she finally grasped his hand and pressed it to her breast, her tight, hard nipple aching with need. He growled against her lips at the bold move, tearing his mouth from hers, eyes popping open to study her.

"I want ye to touch me," she murmured.

Shaw let out a noise that bordered on feral and kissed her again as he massaged her breast. Sensation whipped through her quickly, her body remembering the way this had felt before and causing her to anticipate all the more that crashing wave she wanted so desperately. He tore his mouth from hers and trailed kisses down her neck to her breast, teething her nipple through her gown and then yanking the fabric out of the way to wrap his lips around the turgid peak, sucking in earnest.

Jane cried out, arching her back. Murmuring, "Oh, aye."

As he teased her nipple, his fingers trailed beneath her gown, sliding up her thigh to find her pulsing, hot center.

"Bloody hell, ye're so wet..." he growled against her breasts. "I must taste ye."

To her surprise, he lifted her skirts and ducked beneath, pressing his lips to her thigh. Jane gasped and tried to sit up, to pull him away, but then he breathed on her most sensitive place, and she fell back on a moan. What in heavens...?

Wicked... Oh, how she desired every touch this pirate offered her.

She couldn't think, could only feel as his tongue slid between her slick folds and sent her entire body and mind into a tailspin. "What...? Oh my... Oh!"

Someone banged on the door, and shouts arose from above at the same time her entire body broke apart in that same pleasurable way he'd made her climax before, only this time, more intense. Her body quaked, and he gave her one more long lick, before standing up and going to the door, leaving her there trying to gain a grip on her senses.

He shouted through the wood, "Someone better be dying."

"Come quick, Cap'n. The Spaniards have boarded our ship."

Jane's heart lurched, and all pleasure quickly evaporated and was replaced by fear.

Shaw growled and bit out, "*Los Demonios de Mar.* Ballocks!" He turned to Jane. "Stay here. Bar the door." And then he was gone.

CHAPTER THIRTEEN

ith a cock harder than granite, Shaw marched up on deck to find Captain Santiago Fernandez, of *Los Demonios de Mar*, the Demons of the Sea, standing on his deck. The man was tall, wiry thin, with a long, pointed beard and sharp black eyes that could have been molded from the depths of the deep, deathly sea.

For several breaths, they eyed each other. The tension on the ship pulsed. Santiago had three of his crew standing behind him, their hands on the hilts of their deceptively thin swords. In answer to that subtle, threatening gesture, Shaw's men also had their hands on their weapons, ready to spring at the slightest provocation.

Shaw stared him down, murder in his eyes, gritting his teeth and wishing they were anywhere but here so he could engage the bastard in combat. "Get off my ship."

From the corner of his eye, Shaw watched as Constantine leapt from his own ship onto Shaw's.

"Ye're outnumbered, ye slimy Spanish bastard," Shaw warned. "Back up slowly toward the gangplank and remove yourself."

Santiago grinned cunningly, as though he held a secret. "What are you doing in England?"

"None of your damned business."

The Spanish captain unfurled his fingers and pointed toward the dock. "But I'm certain the Royal Navy would love to know what a bunch of pirates are doing in their port."

"To give me away. Ye'd have to give yourself away. And we both know ye arena going to do that."

Santiago chuckled, though there was no mirth in the sound. "Ah, but you see, I have already paid off the dock master. He allows me passage whenever I please. You, on the other hand, I doubt have done so. He also tells me if there is someone in port who might be of interest. He was very interested in you and your bride, and where you were going. Tell me, where did you go? And where is your woman?"

Shaw gritted his teeth. *Blast it!* He should have thought of that. Of course, Santiago, the slimy whoreson would have spies. Everyone had spies. He kept his face blank and stared the man down. "Ye wouldna get more than three feet from me before I sent ye to Davy Jones's locker, maggot. In fact"— Shaw took a menacing step forward, and at the same time, his men and Constantine's circled the Spanish captain and his three lackeys—"if ye want to make it off my ship alive, I suggest we escort ye and your men back to your ship and see ye untied."

Santiago's lip curled. "You think it will be so easy?"

"I know it will be easy." With a flick of his wrist, Shaw produced the dagger that he always kept up his sleeve and pressed it to the breeches of the Spanish Captain. "Else ye'll be leaving here without your ballocks."

Santiago chuckled as though Shaw had just told the wittiest jest. "You're a savage."

"I live up to my name."

"Get out of my port," Santiago demanded. "Else I'll have my men return to the house you visited to find out why."

Damn, he should have known they'd be followed. He was so intent on keeping Jane safe that his senses had not been keen enough. The woman weakened him. But he couldn't let that show. "This isna *your* port, no matter how much coin ye've paid the dockmaster. If I have to double it, I will to see your greasy arse sink at sea." He pressed the blade tighter, signaling to Jack, who signaled the men, and all of them pulled their swords at once. "Shall I call the dock master over to settle the matter, or will ye be on your way?"

Santiago jerked his head forward and hissed. Shaw wasn't jesting, nor would he allow the bastard to think he didn't mean business. He flicked his hand to the right, slicing the man's breeches at his hip, and cutting him just enough to sting but not do any serious damage.

"Get off my ship," Shaw snarled.

Santiago held up his hands and backed away slowly, nodding to his men to stand down. He might be retreating, but this was by no means over.

"I'd be happy to escort him," Constantine said with a menacing smile and gesturing for a few of his men to board the *Savage of the Sea*.

"What kind of ally would I be to take that away from ye?" Shaw said, swiping the black velvet hat from Santiago's head.

"You've not seen the last of me, ye Scottish dung heap."

Shaw chuckled as though he'd not a care in the world. "See ye at sea."

Santiago glowered, murder in his eyes. They'd always been enemies, but this was war. After Shaw helped Constantine take care of the French, he'd have to ask his English ally to help eradicate the Spaniards, too. Not that Constantine would mind. The two of them loved a good battle, and whenever they teamed up, they were unstoppable. Which is why, perhaps, they preferred to keep their alliance, for if either one of them went up against each other, there was no telling what kind of damage would be done. The immeasurable kind.

Shaw watched them go down the docks but caught movement to the left of his ship, which sent a prickle of apprehension up his spine. Was Santiago a distraction for a greater attack? Instantly, he recognized Jane's Uncle Edward, though he stood quietly in the shadows. Standing beside him was a tall, broad man with a menacing look about him, and a young lad of perhaps fifteen or sixteen summers.

His first impression of Alexander, the supposed King of Scotland, was that he was lacking. There was a hunted look to him as his gaze darted about. He would have been noticed right away at a boxing match, and Shaw concluded right then and there, that they had not been at a boxing match at all. Despite the hunted demeanor, Alexander was nothing compared to the lad of ten Shaw had seen five years ago when he met Jane. To think that grown men had to bow to a prideful child who knew nothing of running a country really made him shake his head. And here was yet another poor, weak lad being used as a pawn in a great game of men. But the closer they drew to Shaw, the more he realized that this boy king had none of the boastful pride of his brother. There was an earnest look about him. Alexander didn't know if he was going to live or die. Always on the run. Always looking over his shoulder. That ate at a man, let alone a lad. They reached the bottom of the gangway, heads bowed, the hoods of their cloaks concealing parts of their faces.

"Welcome to the *Savage of the Sea*," Shaw said, sweeping his arm wide and indicating they should walk up the gangway.

They made their way up, and Shaw gifted the lad with Santiago's hat. The lad didn't grin, but he did nod his head, and a spark of interest flashed in his eyes as he regarded the ship and the men on it, including Shaw. A bit of the cautious haze around his eyes slipped away, replaced by an inner strength that longed to be set free. He reminded Shaw a little of himself at that age.

Edward glowered, hands fisted at his side as he took in the ship and the men on it. "Where is Lady Jane?"

"She's in her cabin." Shaw kept his gaze on the man, feeling the vibrations of his anger, and checked sideways at Lorne—who had the moniker Black Knight for a reason.

"Good. She doesna need to hear what I have to say." Edward came close, perhaps a foot or less away from Shaw, though the affect was not as he had likely wished considering he was a good half a foot shorter than Shaw and not nearly as broad. "Ye're a bloody pirate. Is your name even Shaw MacDougall?"

Shaw grinned with pride, swept off his hat and bowed low. "Aye. But my friends and enemies call me Captain Savage, Prince of the Devils of the Deep."

Edward's frown narrowed, while the lad's brightened.

But it wasn't Uncle Edward he had to worry about, for the Black Knight decided to live up to his name. He pulled from a scabbard a blade as long as a man that glinted in the moonlight off the sharpness of its tip. The sound of metal sliding from scabbards was heard all around, as well as the grumble of excitement from Shaw's men. They loved a good fight, though this one would prove to be less than exciting given it was three against thirty.

"Let us leave," Edward said, taking note of the number of swords pointed at his throat.

"I am not holding ye hostage." Shaw's grin held no bit of joviality, but of warning.

Edward kept his gaze steady on Shaw. "Then why did ye send for us?"

Telling the truth wouldn't hurt. "Livingstone will soon find ye."

"How do ye know?"

"Because he found Jane. And it's only a matter of time before he finds ye. His reach is wide, and ye, Sir Lorne, are known about parliament. For the right price, which Livingstone is willing to pay, ye will be found."

"So ye would take us hostage instead?"

Shaw frowned. "Nay."

"Then why are ye trying to help us? And dinna insult me by saying 'tis for my dear niece. I dinna know how ye convinced her to marry ye, but 'twas a feat of evil I'm certain. What did ye do? Seduce her? Imprison her and impregnate her?"

Shaw winged a brow. "As a matter of fact, Jane asked me to marry her." Blast, but that felt good to say.

Edward let out a bark of laughter. "I'd not seek employment as a jester any time soon, ye wastrel, for your jests are not at all entertaining."

"I assure ye, I dinna lie." Of course, Shaw wasn't going to tell the bastard that he'd told her she needed to grace his bed and marriage was the only way she'd agree to that. Even now, he could still taste her on his tongue. How desperately he wanted to go back to the cabin and finish what they'd started. For the first time, she'd surrendered to him. Confessed she wanted him to touch her. Ballocks, but his cock was swiftly growing hard again. Shaking himself out of his stupor, he said, "But ye're welcome to ask the lass yourself."

"How can I trust anything she says if she'd be so willing to align herself with a pirate—forced or nay. What kind of spell did ye put on her?"

Shaw put his sword away and crossed his arms over his chest. Time for Edward to know a little bit more of the truth.

They needed to get moving, for the longer they stayed in port, the more chances they had of discovery. "Are ye aware that I'm the one who took her to Iona five years ago?"

At that, Edward blanched, exchanging a glance with Lorne. "Ye lie."

"Nay." Shaw stared them in the eyes, deadly serious as he spoke in low tones. "I was at Edinburgh Castle for the deadly feast, hired as a mercenary by Livingstone." Perhaps keeping his role in the desired murder of Jane a secret was a good idea. "When I saw one of the bastard guards go after Lady Jane, I followed. Stopped him in mid—" He swallowed past his fury at envisioning that whoreson attempting to rape her. "Stopped him from assaulting her, which would have led to her death. I took her from there. And when I asked her where she wanted to go, she said to her aunt in Iona."

Edward nodded, suspicion clearing from his vision. "My sister."

"When she found out that Livingstone was planning to visit the abbey, she sent for me. Told me she needed my help."

"And ye obliged willingly?" Lorne had not lost his skeptical glower. "What did she offer ye? And dinna tell me 'twas marriage."

Shaw glanced at the lad. "Besides the satisfaction of thwarting Livingstone again, she advised me that I'd be securing the greatest treasure in the land."

"So ye do plan to hold the lad hostage."

"Nay. But I will be accepting a high price in gold for safe transport. Call me your personal guarded escort. And trust me, Livingstone will never get to Alexander if he's in my care."

"And where exactly will ye take the lad?"

"Is there no place that ye think will be safe?" Shaw asked.

Edward's shoulders sagged, and he glanced at Lorne. "Nay."

"Then until ye find a place, perhaps 'tis best for the lad to come with me to my island, Scarba."

Edward frowned. "And what of us?"

Shaw swept his arm toward the gangway. "The two of ye are free to go."

"We've both made a vow to protect the lad with our lives." Lorne glanced at Alexander with surprising affection for man of such deadly reputation. "My wife, his late mother, bade me promise, and I could never break that promise to her, even in death."

"Then ye shall accompany us," Shaw said. "Edward?"

"I will not leave them, or my niece. My brother would never forgive me. Once we reach Scarba, I will escort her and the lad back to Crawford Castle."

"There's a reason she's not been there all this time. 'Tis not safe. And I believe Lorne will agree with me."

"'Tis a family matter, and we will take care of it," Edward spat. "Her father needs to know she is safe. Word will soon reach him she's no longer safely in Rome."

Jane was blessed to have a father who cared for her. Shaw's father had thrown him away without a backward glance, and no doubt, Jane's father had been fearful of her safety for the last five years. But that didn't mean the man would be the safest choice for her, and definitely not the safest for the lad.

"Rome?"

"Aye. That is where her aunt said she was, so that not even her father would know she was on Iona."

Shaw grunted. "I will not allow ye to take either one of them. That is the first place they will look. Livingstone still found her, even when very few people knew where she sought sanctuary previously."

"Except a pirate." Edward eyed him skeptically. "She wanted to keep her whereabouts a secret. My sister had

138

vowed not to say a word, else Livingstone would have information he could hold over my brother's head."

"And it would seem your plan did not work."

Edward ignored him. "And when I learned she was there, I, too, vowed to keep her secret."

"How did ye know to go to the abbey in Iona, Lorne?" Shaw asked the Black Knight.

The deadly Scottish knight crossed his arms over his chest. "Divine intervention."

"I dinna believe in such." Shaw pierced him with a glower, and Edward repeated the sentiments.

"My niece, Maria, told us to go there to seek sanctuary. When we were there, we found Jane, though she was called Marina. All the same, I recognized her as the Countess of Douglas, albeit a wee bit older."

The name Maria sparked something in Shaw's memory. He recalled a Maria in Jane's letters. She was suspicious of the woman. And now, if it was the same lass, her name was resurfacing. He'd have to ask Jane about it. Saints, but his wife had risked much to see to Alexander's safety.

Shaw was doubly impressed by all his wee wife had done to secure a lad she barely knew. And he was also hugely aware that he did not deserve her. She was strong, patriotic, and a lady. He was nothing but a scurvy pirate without a hint of morals, beyond saving the only lass who'd touched his heart.

"I will take her to her father," Shaw said. "After I take care of Livingstone."

Edward squared his shoulders, fury in his eyes. "Nay. This sham of a marriage will be dissolved, and I will take her back to safety myself."

"Our marriage was not a sham," Shaw countered.

"Of course ye'd see to it that ye had her in your clutches." Edward was sputtering, hands fisted at his sides again.

If the man didn't calm down, he was apt to have a fit of apoplexy.

"Ye know nothing of me." There wasn't a hint of offense in Shaw's tone. He was a pirate. A brutal man. And he'd be willing to bet that at least half the things Edward must be thinking about him were indeed true.

"Uncle, I will not go back to Crawford Castle. My place is by my husband's side." Jane's voice startled Shaw from his deliberations on whether or not it would be a good idea to toss Edward from the ship, just to watch him splutter in the water as he did on dry land.

"Dear Jane, go back to the cabin," Edward ordered.

Though Shaw didn't like the tone Edward took one bit, at least they agreed. "Aye, go back, lass."

But instead of listening, Jane descended from the stairs that led up to the captain's quarters above deck, her emotions full on her face—anger and determination.

"Uncle, I'm glad ye've come. We must secure Alexander's safety. That is our task. That is our most *important* task. For the good of the country. And to do so, we have to align ourselves with powerful allies. I have done that. And I will not back away from my vows, even when this task is complete."

Edward was turning purple now. "Ye would be the wife of a blackguard? A pirate?"

Jane glanced up at Shaw, pride in her eyes. "I would be the wife of Shaw MacDougall, aye."

"A pirate." Edward stomped his foot.

But Jane's voice was calm, her eyes grazing over Shaw like a soft caress. "He's much more than a pirate to me, and there is nothing ye can do about it, Uncle. Please, accept this. Shaw and I will tell my father when this business with Prince Alexander is handled." She dipped into a curtsy. "Apologies for not greeting ye sooner."

The prince's face flamed red. "No need for apologies, my lady. Ye are beautiful."

Shaw raised a brow at that, and then it was Jane's turn to blush.

"Thank ye verra much for saying so."

"While continuing this conversation would be quite diverting for us all, we need to set sail," Shaw said. "We've already had an encounter with the Spaniards, and Livingstone is likely due to arrive in port any hour now."

Shaw nodded toward Constantine's ship. "We'll have an escort through the English channel. But only if we dinna dally."

Edward and Lorne exchanged glances once more and then agreed to accept Shaw's help—but not before informing him the likelihood of gold was nil. So instead, Shaw negotiated a lifetime of pardons for all the brethren, which Lorne agreed to relay to the right channels.

CHAPTER FOURTEEN

ot since the night they'd spent in the castle on the Isle of Scarba had Shaw come to share the bed with Jane, so after she'd washed her face, changed into her nightrail and slipped beneath the covers, she was surprised when the door to the cabin rattled. She'd barred it every night as Shaw had bid her. A brief moment of panic that they'd been boarded and she'd not heard it washed through her mind.

Slipping from bed, she crossed the cabin silently, her toes growing colder with each step.

"Jane." Shaw's voice came through the door.

Jane startled. What was he doing here? Had something happened?

Without hesitation, she raised the bar and opened the door, backing away for him, allowing him space to enter. She crossed her arms over her chest to hide her breasts, which were visible through the chemise. Though, thankfully, the only light in the room was that of the moon shining through the porthole.

"Lass," he said slowly, his gaze raking over her. "I didna mean to wake ye."

"I hadna yet fallen asleep." Her voice sounded throaty all the sudden, taking on that wispy sound it had when she... when they... Heat crept into her cheeks, and she looked down at the floor to see her toes curling and his boots, large and impressive, like him.

"I'm sorry still to have made ye rise." He backed toward the door.

Jane raised her eyes to meet his. "Dinna be sorry, Shaw. This is your ship, your cabin."

"And ye're my wife."

"Aye."

"What ye said...to your uncle, in front of the whole crew..."

She squared her shoulders, prepared for him to tell her it wasn't going to work out. That what she'd done was inappropriate. That once more, she'd disobeyed a direct order to stay inside their cabin. That as soon as he was done with Alexander, he would allow her to leave with her uncle, that to do so would be best. Indeed, she was certain most of the men on this ship might agree.

And perhaps she would have agreed a few days before.

But she didn't think so anymore, and that was why she'd said it. When she'd heard the men arguing, she'd left the cabin without thinking to inform her uncle she would not be going anywhere, because the very idea of leaving Shaw, of not having him in her life, seemed preposterous.

Aye, that likely made her seem witless, and perhaps she was, but something had happened over the past few days. Something that had been brewing between them for several years now. She couldn't simply throw that away, toss it to the windblown sea and turn her back.

Her tongue felt thick. There was nothing to say, other than, "I meant it."

"Why?" He started to walk toward her, the moon catching the emerald glint in his eyes.

They were beautiful, mesmerizing, glittering jewels, and full of…need. Desire, aye, but something more intense than that. A need that reached between them and tugged at a place in her chest she'd never identified before. And that place that pulsed within her ribs leapt out with its own need, grasping tightly to the virtual rope that bound them.

Jane took a step back, needing space to breathe, to think, to answer. Because the closer he drew, the less her mind seemed capable of rational thought, the more she wanted to stare at his mouth and think about his hands on her body. The more she wanted to surrender. To give herself completely.

"Tell me, lass," he murmured. "Why did ye say it? I am a pirate, how could I be more than a pirate to ye?"

"Your profession does not make ye who ye are."

"Who am I?" Another step forward.

Another step in retreat.

Jane lifted her chin, meeting his gaze and feeling as though she'd been struck by some invisible, tingling force. "Ye're a man of honor."

"There is no honor among thieves." Saints, but his voice was so smooth. So melodic it was spellbinding, enchanting.

"But ye are. With me, at least."

"Is that so?"

"Tell me an instance in which ye havena been."

A slow grin curled his lips, and he took another step closer. When Jane went to retreat, her knees hit the mattress, and for a second, she thought she might tumble backward. He seemed to take pity on her for the moment and didn't close the distance, allowing her to regain her balance.

"Och, lass, in my thoughts, in the dark of night, in the bright of day, when I think about my hands on your skin." He reached out and brushed his fingers up her arm, leaving goosebumps in their wake. "When I think of my mouth on your lips." He brushed his thumb over her lower lip and then dragged it down her neck, over her chest and between her breasts. "My tongue on your nipples." He cupped her breast. "When I think of how ye let me kiss your sweet honey." He did close the distance then, pressing the hard length of himself between her thighs. Unbidden, she quivered, a sudden shudder making her legs squeeze tight. Her breath hitched. "My thoughts are not at all honorable when I'm thinking about ye, love. About how I want to feel ye quiver on my tongue again. How I want to thrust deep inside ye, claim ye once and for all."

Oh God! The things he was saying. The low, husky timbre of his voice... How was she going to be able to breathe? To talk? To stand? She wanted to rip off her nightrail and beg him to take her. To make her feel all those things. To make her his.

"I am your wife, Shaw," she managed to say without choking. "How does that make your thoughts dishonorable?"

Shaw groaned. "Because I made ye a promise."

"And—" She bit her lip, swallowed hard. "What if I say I take it back?"

His eyelids dipped closed briefly, the muscle in his jaw ticking, hands at her hips tightening, and the turgid steel pressed to her nether regions appeared to grow all the harder.

"Ye must tell me explicitly, love, for I dare not do anything ye dinna want."

"Make me yours, Shaw. Make your wife in truth."

"Specifically," he demanded, his voice so low deep and gravelly she wanted to cry out in pleasure from it.

Instead, she reached for the ribbons of her chemise and undid them as he watched, the soft linen falling open to reveal the space between her breasts, all the way to her navel. Shaw's nostrils flared as he watched her, his lips pressed firmly together, body rigid.

Jane took it a step farther, tugging the chemise from her shoulders and letting the fabric fall in a pool of linen at her feet. She stood before him completely nude. The leather of his breeches warm against her thighs, the linen of his shirt tickling her belly.

"I want ye to make love to me," she said.

"There will be no going back," he warned.

"I never want to go back."

Still, he stood rigid, as if he didn't believe her. "I will not change. I will not suddenly develop a conscience and become a lord of the court. I will not give up my ships."

"I would never ask that of ye."

"Ye would spend your days at Scarba."

Jane tugged at the laces on his shirt. "I will be the best mistress the castle has ever had."

"My job is dangerous. I could die." He pressed his hand over hers, stilling her, pressing her palm to his strong heartbeat.

"So is the life of a warrior, Shaw."

"I could be arrested."

She raised a brow in challenge. The man could come up with every reason under the sun, but she wasn't going to let him go that easy. "Then ye'd best have a plan of escape."

"Ye have an answer for everything."

"I know what I want."

"Why would ye want me?" There was such turmoil in his voice, the pain of his past coming to the surface as he lay open his heart to her.

"Because, Shaw MacDougall, my gentle warrior, I *love* ye."

His answer was a guttural moan. He cupped both sides of her face and bent to kiss her, emotion flowing between the two of them in that heated kiss. She didn't need him to tell her how he felt, she could feel it in her bones, and in the way he kissed her. In the way he'd protected her all these years. The way he respected her. The way he wanted to make sure she really wanted this, wanted him.

Jane circled her arms around his neck, sinking her naked body against him, giving herself completely and whole-heartedly.

Shaw slid his arms around her back, trailing his fingers up and down her spine as he kissed her. The light, feathery touch was powerful, sending shivers coursing through every limb, and an ache to settle deep in her loins. God, how she needed him, needed this.

Squirming against him, she tugged at his shirt, wanting to know what it would feel like to have skin-to-skin contact, to press her breasts to his chest. She let out a soft moan as he slid his hands down to her bottom, cupping her and lifting her.

"Lay down on the bed, love. We're going to do this properly."

She did as he asked, watching as he took off his clothes. First his shirt, exposing all that muscle. A sprinkle of dark hair covered his chest and led in a sensual line beneath the breeches he'd worn to look more English when they'd disembarked.

"Ye're beautiful," she murmured, rolling onto her side and propping her head up on her bent arm to get a better view.

Shaw snickered. "No one has ever called me beautiful."

"Then they must have been speechless from the magnificence of your physique."

He chuckled at that, tugging off his boots and hose. For a moment, he stood in only his breeches, his breaths coming more labored than they usually did as he perused her, raking her with his hot gaze.

"Are ye certain?" he asked.

Jane did not hesitate to answer. "Aye."

His eyes darkened in the moonlight, and even she swore the pulse in his neck leapt. Was he as nervous as she was? Reaching for the laces of his breeches, he started to untie them, revealing inch by inch the hardness that had rubbed so tantalizingly against her. Just as she'd seen that first night, she took in his shaft—long, thick, hard and jutting forward like a battering ram. Was that what it would be like? A battering ram as he laid siege to her body and broke down all of her barriers?

Nay, not with the way he'd touched her, kissed her. He was gentle in his ministrations, if not passionate. Never punitive. She trusted that his lovemaking would be the same.

Shaw approached the bed, and she scooted back, giving him space to lie down beside her. The mattress dipped with the weight of his knee pressing down upon it, and then he was crawling over her, swiftly taking one of her legs and pressing her knee up around his hip, allowing him to settle between her thighs.

The abrupt contact of his body stretched out on hers was dizzying. He was hard where she was soft. The hairs on his chest and legs tickled, but what was most different was the hard, pulsing length of him pressed intimately to the folds between her thighs. A fresh rush of need surged in her veins.

They both let out a moan, eyes locked on one another.

"There is still time to turn back," Shaw warned.

"I'm not turning back."

Shaw grinned. "Good. Because I want ye, lass. I want ye more than I've ever wanted anything in my life."

Her heart fluttered in her chest. That was as near an

admission of love as she was likely to get. "I love ye," she said. "I love ye so much."

Shaw silenced her declaration with a heated kiss, intense enough to steal her breath and send her heart into palpitations. She clung to him, fingers clutching the rippling muscles of his shoulders, legs to his hips, feet sliding up and down his calves. God, he felt so good. Incredible. Wondrous.

This was right. They were right.

The more he kissed her, caressed her, the more determined she was. Her body was on fire with longing, passion. He trailed his lips over her skin, taking her nipples into the heat of his mouth and tormenting her with his tongue. Jane writhed beneath him, the pressure she'd felt when he touched her before was building at a rapid pace, and the more she squirmed, the more she wanted.

Shaw dipped his fingers between her legs, sliding over her folds and then inside her. She arched her back, begging him with her moans for... What? She was quick to find out, when she felt the tip of his massive manhood touch her opening, but he stilled without going forward.

Sensing he was awaiting her permission, she slid her hands down his back to cup his muscular rear and lifted her hips. It was all the encouragement he needed. He surged forward, driving deep. Pain ripped her inside and out. She gasped, struggling against him, only causing the uncomfortable intensity to increase as he filled her, stretched her.

Jane stilled suddenly, praying he was through, that their mating was complete. When she opened her eyes, Shaw stared down at her in shock and horror.

"Ye're a bloody virgin."

Her eyes widened, and Jane realized she probably should have told him that before, but...it hadn't come up, and then she'd not thought about it. In their passion, she'd forgotten completely that he didn't know. Heat flamed her face. Why hadn't she told him?

"Aye," she whispered.

Shaw's forehead pressed to hers, his breathing labored. "I'm sorry for hurting ye. I would have been more careful. Dammit. Bloody hell..." He let out a few more curses, bringing her to the point of tears. "God, Jane." He kissed her tears, her forehead. "I'm so sorry. We dinna have to continue. I'll leave ye alone."

"I'm sorry for not telling ye. I'm sorry for disappointing ye."

"Och, love, ye didna disappoint me. Never. I'm frustrated with myself. I'm a monster." He shifted to move away from her, but just that subtle movement sent a wave of something pleasurable through her.

The pain had gone without her realizing it, replaced with a heavy feeling of wanting. "There is no pain. Not anymore. Dinna stop."

Shaw let out a ragged breath. "Are ye certain?"

She wriggled beneath him, and he groaned. "Aye."

"Thank God." He kissed her hard, sweat dripping down the sides of his temple. "Ye feel too good to stop. Now, ye're truly mine. All mine." Gradually, he pulled out and then, with agonizing slowness, pushed back in.

Jane moaned at the intensified pleasure. "Please, dinna stop."

"I want to make ye come. I want to feel ye shudder around me." Shaw whispered in her ear, low, gravelly, sensual as he moved, pulling out and plunging back in. He kissed her, caressed her, gripped her buttocks and lifted her to go deeper, thrusting hard, fast, slow, gentle... His pace was meant to bring her to the brink and then toy with her, teasing her. And then he didn't stop. Driving deep and hard again and again until she felt that same brilliant explosion that he'd given her with his mouth, his fingers. Jane cried out, arching her back and moving her hips to ride out the pleasure.

"*Mo chreach*," Shaw groaned, and then he, too, was shuddering.

They lay covered in a sheen of sweat, their bodies still connected, their breaths heavy.

"Did I please ye?" she asked, worried that he might still be upset with her.

"Aye, love. More than pleased me."

"And ye're not mad at me?"

"Ye did nothing wrong." He rolled to the side taking her with him. "Ye're perfect. I'd not change a thing about ye."

CHAPTER FIFTEEN

S haw woke in the middle of the night to an intense explosion that rocked the ship and drilled his ears. The shock of the boom was quickly followed by the shouts of his men. He leapt from bed, grabbed his breeches and tugged them on as he ran for the door to their cabin and burst through it.

The men on the deck were running like mad. Flames rose from the bow where they'd been hit, and swabs rushed with buckets to put it out. Smoke curled into the night air, mixing with the scent of panic.

Certain it was the Spaniards, Shaw was surprised to see the flag of the French pirates flying high. Blood red, the shape of a skeletal king with a *fleur-de-lis* hilted sword was painted on its surface

"Les Porteurs D'eau." The Water Bearers. French in origin, their current leader was a Flemish blackguard who was more ruthless and cutthroat than Shaw imagined the Devil himself would be, only this one dressed like a king, and wore a crown over his close-cropped dark hair.

"Nous sommes venus pour vous. Il n'y a nulle part où se

cacher." Nicolas Van Rompay hung from the yardarm, swinging his sword in the air as he shouted those words meant to threaten Shaw and his men, "We've come for you. There is nowhere to hide."

Shaw let out a string of oaths. Chaos reigned, but at least his men were being efficient. Swabs put out the fires as the other crew fought hard with the bloody French crawling over his ship like ants on a tasty morsel. Somehow, in the middle of the night, Van Rompay and his men had been able to quietly creep up to their ship and blow out a part of his bow with their cannon as well as part of the hull that the men below were trying to quickly salvage before the ship started to take on water. French pirates swarmed the deck, fighting without mercy against the Devils of the Deep.

Why the hell had the French attacked at night? And then he knew, they'd been nearing the Cornwall coast as they sailed. They were nearly to Perran. The French must have been planning an attack at the Poseidon's Legion stronghold. They'd intercepted Shaw when they saw his flag, knowing that they had an alliance with the English.

Van Rompay gave a sharp order in French that sent a ripple of dread down Shaw's spine. He glanced up just in time to see two heavily muscled pirates gripping onto the rigging they'd cut from one of Shaw's masts, flying through the air with Lorne and Alexander in their grips.

"Bastards!" Shaw growled. He reached for his sword, but it wasn't on his hip. In his haste to leave his cabin, he'd not grabbed any weapons. And while he normally slept fully armored on the ship, last night he'd fallen into a deep sleep nude and in the arms of his wife.

Doing so had left him vulnerable. Weak. The very thing he feared the most. At every turn, Jane left him exposed to his enemies, and because of that, they were all in danger. If he'd been sleeping on the deck as he had the previous two nights, he might have spotted the enemy before they were upon them.

"Cap'n!" Jack tossed him a sword, and Shaw leapt onto the rail of the ship, prepared to leap over the black yawning water and onto the French pirate ship when a distinct cry from his wife cut the air.

Hearing her cry of fear and pain sliced him to the quick.

He knew without looking that one of the French bastard's men would have her. Even still, when he turned to take her in, the sight of the blade at her beautiful naked neck was more than he could take. It was a crushing image.

The lass was his Achilles' heel, and he would be the death of her.

Shaw fought the urge to bellow as he swept his gaze over his wife who stood there completely naked, the moonlight shining off her creamy skin, clashing against the blackguard's arm around her neck and waist. Anger flashed in her eyes. Fear, too, but the latter was drowned out by the ferocious-ness of her gritted teeth.

Fury pummeled his insides. How dare that bastard touch his wife? As soon as he got the chance, he was going to gut that man and personally feed him to the sharks.

"A lady, that is not what we expected to find on your ship," Van Rompay called in his nasally French accent from where he perched in the crow's nest high up on the mast of his ship. "How very fortunate *pour moi*, and unfortunate *pour vous*."

"Get your hands off her," Shaw growled, ignoring Van Rompay. "Else meet your death."

In answer, the cretin's hand searched out Jane's breast. She kept her eyes on Shaw, never wavering, her teeth showing in her grimace of rage.

He wanted to chop the bastard's head off, to rip off his arms and shove them down the stump. But he stood, motionless as he tried to figure out what to do. Aye, he'd not been able to tell her before, but looking at her now, seeing her fear, feeling it beat against his own, he knew that he loved her. Deeply.

Which solidified his deep-seated belief that love weakened a man.

Look at him now, unable to move, trying to decide between his men, his ship and a mere slip of a girl who had clutched his heart five years before. Since the day he'd seen her on the floor of that bedchamber, his entire world had been changed. He no longer allowed his men to plunder, even if he'd never indulged in the act himself. Something in her eyes had broken him—though at the time, he'd felt more alive than ever.

Just like he had last night when he'd laid claim to her himself, when he'd made her his in truth. And when he'd imagined kidnapping a priest from the nearest port and squirreling him away to Scarba to marry them in the eyes of God and all, and to remain there should his wife need a confessor. She had spent the last five years at an abbey after all, and he couldn't let her drop everything simply because of who and what he was.

But now, there she stood, a shining beacon of all that he was—a weak, foolish man. And yet, he loved her, and knowing that, how it made him vulnerable, didn't change how he felt. But he wasn't going to let her, or his men, go down because of his wayward heart. He had a duty as their captain, their prince, as her husband. To protect them. See them all safe, and the only way to do that was to…deny her.

"Surrender, and ye shall have her back." Van Rompay appeared close by, having risked coming down from his perch to witness Shaw's surrender. The wry quirk of the French captain's brow made Shaw want to commit murder. The man thought Shaw would drop to his knees and beg.

From behind the French ship was a flicker of motion. Shaw kept his gaze steady on Van Rompay as he watched Constantine's ship sail from beneath the fog of night to flank the French ship's starboard side.

The Gaia was silent as she slithered through the water like a beast seeking its prey. The men onboard the French ship had their attention so wrapped up in their captain and the naked lass, they had no clue that Shaw's English allies would soon be upon them. And he would give them no quarter.

Shaw scoffed, let out a bitter laugh that sounded false to his own ears. "Surrender for that mere slip of a woman? Ha! Ye'll have to do better than that, French scum. I barely know her. She means nothing to me. A harlot I picked up in London."

And then he did the most painful thing imaginable—he turned his back on her, unwilling to see how deep his words cut. But that didn't mean he couldn't feel her steely gaze boring into his spine. If they were alone, he had no doubt she would scratch his eyes out, and he deserved it.

She'd given herself to him, and he'd taken what she offered—with relish, again and again—and now he was betraying her. Or at least, she would believe he was betraying her, and that was all that mattered. He needed her to hate him in order to save her life.

"Then ye willna care if I take her with me?" Van Rompay shouted.

Shaw didn't falter in his stance, even if every muscle and organ inside twitched. Dear God, if Shaw could breathe fire he would. He waved his hand, not trusting his own voice when he raged inside at the sight of her being touched by another, harmed by another.

At that moment, the French seemed to have regained their senses, taking note of the English ship flanking their others side. With a hiss of fury, Van Rompay turned away from Jane and ordered his men to fire their cannon's on *The Gaia*. Even from here, Shaw could hear Constantine's laugh, as he opened fire on the French ship.

Great booms followed by the splintering of wood and the cries of men where heard, and Shaw let out an expletive. If they blew the French ship to hell, it would take the Black Knight and Alexander with it.

"Cease, le Brecque!" Shaw bellowed. "They have Lorne!"

Across the sea, Constantine cursed, having caught Shaw's message on the wind. He called for a ceasefire, and instead had his men send grappling hooks over the French rail, tugging her in.

Shaw turned a deadly grin on the man holding his wife.

The bastard was still gritting his teeth, clutching Jane's breast. A prickle of blood trailed down her neck from where the man had pricked her skin. That tiny trickle was enough to send Shaw into a blinding rage.

He flung his arm out with precision, sending the dagger he'd jerked off a dead man flying. Before the bastard could figure out what was happening, the tip of the dagger was tunneling into his eye. He screamed, his fingers tightening on Jane and the knife he held at her throat, but Shaw was quicker. As soon as he'd let his dagger fly, he'd shifted to the right in one quick step and brought his sword down on the man's elbow, causing him to drop the knife.

The French pirate crumpled, his life extinguished, and while his thick weight and grip would have taken Jane with him, Shaw reached out his free hand for her and took her up against him, her naked breasts cold from the night air and her fear against his heated chest.

He gazed down at her intensely, knowing that she was his breath as well as his doom. Opening his mouth, he wanted to tell her he was sorry. That he'd warned her the life of a pirate's wife was dangerous, deadly, but the words stilled on his tongue as he took in the angry set of her mouth, the coldness in her eyes.

"Get your hands off me," she growled. Her eyes were cold, her voice like ice.

"Jane—" he started, but she cut him off, bringing the heel of her tiny foot down on his bare toes.

The move hardly hurt at all, but he knew the reaction she wanted, and because it hit him in the chest, he did wince.

"Ye were right," she seethed. "We dinna suit. I will return to my father with my uncle." Wrenching away from him was easy, given his arms seemed to have gone numb, his brain blank.

He watched, speechless as she ran back toward their cabin, and he moved too late to cover her, but he had nothing to give her anyhow. By the time she was through the door, he'd barely reached the stairs.

Blood rushed in and out of his ears. But the slice of blade on his arm had him turning, reengaging in full on battle. The wound he sustained was not deep and did not hamper his fighting abilities. He came at his enemies like the Savage he was, letting them know just why his crew was named the Devils of the Deep. He let all the anger he felt at what had happened to Jane and how he'd had to hurt her come out in the blade of his sword.

Shaw had cut down five men before Van Rompay called a retreat.

"No mercy!" Shaw bellowed.

But then Van Rompay bellowed Shaw's name, showing him that he held Alexander with a knife at his throat at the bow of the French ship. "Let us go, or I will kill your treasure."

Shaw, knowing just how savage the French were, had no doubt that Van Rompay would gut the lad and force feed his insides to Lorne.

"Allow them safe passage," Shaw called to his men. To Constantine he said, "Our agreement still holds."

Constantine nodded, calling for his men to back away and to remove the grappling hooks from the French ship. Those French pirates still left alive on Shaw's ship leapt aboard their own, and a within moments, the ships were floating away from each other.

"Ye must truly love her."

Shaw jerked at the sound of Jane's uncle standing beside him. "What?"

"To have given her up like that, ye must love her."

"Is that a jest?"

Uncle Edward shook his head. "I could see the turmoil in your eyes. I know what ye meant to do."

Shaw narrowed his eyes. He barely knew himself, how could Edward Lindsay?

"'Tis a moot point and one easily solved. We were hand-fasted, there is no marriage set in stone, and ye heard her. She will return with ye to her father."

"Dinna be a fool, Savage."

Shaw gritted his teeth. "Letting her go would be the opposite of foolish."

Uncle Edward only shook his head, walking away, leaving Shaw to wonder what the hell he meant as he turned to get his ship back in order.

CHAPTER SIXTEEN

*J*ane was dressing so quickly she actually tore the cuff on her sleeve when she yanked it hard against an opposing force—which happened to be her thumb, and now smarted with pain.

"Blast him!" The unladylike curse rolled awkwardly off her tongue but felt so very good when she shouted it out, relieving a little of the tension in her shoulders. So she tried one of the more vulgar terms she'd heard a crewman say that was far too offensive to put in writing, and that lightened her mood all the more.

How could he have said those things about her in front of everyone? A worthless wench he'd picked up in London? A harlot? Well, so much for cursing, because now her shoulders were ten times tenser. She'd been naked, her body exposed to everyone, and with his words, her humiliation was complete.

After she finished pulling on her boots and a cloak, sufficiently covered from head to toe, not an inch of skin showing, save for her hands, face and part of her neck, she braided her hair and then wrenched open the door to her cabin. In her haste to escape, to remove herself from any thought of

Shaw MacDougall, the true Savage he'd shown her he was, she had completely forgotten that there was, in fact, no escape. The scents of the salty-sea air, smoke and blood whipped at her with the wind generated from their quick sailing toward Perran.

The captain's quarters were on the quarterdeck, a half-dozen steps up from the main deck, and so coming out of the door, she was immediately faced with the crew, and right below her, Shaw at the helm.

Nay, no longer *Shaw* to her, but *Savage*.

She wanted to rake him over the coals, tie him to the mast and whip him as he deserved, the bloody scoundrel. How could he have used her so ill? And how could she have allowed herself to be swept away by foolish, sentimental feelings? To fall in love with him? To admit such love to him…

How mortifying! He'd probably laughed at her when she said it, for he certainly had not returned the sentiment.

Och, more the fool her. This was her own fault.

She'd fallen in love with him years ago and allowed that naïve girl's fantasy to bloom into something ridiculous and so farfetched she was surprised she'd not seen it sooner. But sometimes it took a lash of betrayal for one to see the truth.

And now she saw it. Aye, her eyes were wide open.

She'd married a pirate. Nay, handfasted. But in the eyes of Scottish law, it was legal and binding. But it didn't matter, she'd given him the greatest bargaining chip she had—and that didn't even include her virginity.

Savage, prince of the Devils of the Deep had well and truly plundered her. Taken the treasure she'd held secret and safe for five years—and promptly lost it—and her innocence all in a few day's time.

She had nothing left now.

Turning from the wide, wooden wheel, he glanced up at her. Shame etched in his tragically beautiful emerald eyes.

Regret, too. Seeing that sorrow, part of her heart clenched, wanting to reach out to him, to tell him all would be well, but she couldn't do that. She had to harden her heart against him. Any regret he might feel was likely because she would no longer allow him into her bed. And the shame? Perhaps that came from having tied himself to her in the first place.

He'd never told her he loved her. She'd only been reading into things like a foolish, lovesick idiot. Any passion and emotion she'd felt in his kiss had only been lust. If he cared for her, he would not have turned his back while that vile pirate touched her. He would not have said those horrible things about her, been willing to give her up.

She'd given him what he wanted, and he had no use for her anymore. Hadn't he said all those years ago that one day he would return to reclaim the debt? This whole situation was about that, and nothing else. The debt had been paid in full.

The pain of humiliation and betrayal sank deep into her heart. Why had he saved her all those years ago? Better that she would have perished along with everyone else. Better that she not know what it felt like for a pirate's weapon to pierce her soul.

"Drop me off at the nearest port, Savage," she demanded, standing over him, chin high, and looking down on him as though he were a lowly, wicked servant and she his master.

"Nay." He turned away from her and faced the sea, seemingly undisturbed by her demands.

Her belly clenched, threatening to toss up what meager contents it contained, but still she stood strong. "I demand ye drop me at the nearest port."

Savage slammed his hand on the wheel with a cracking sound, and she was surprised to see that he'd not split the wood. "I said nay, dammit."

Her mouth fell open at his tone, the words. "Why? Why

will ye not let me go?" She couldn't help the anguish in her tone.

"Because the nearest port is there." He pointed toward Perran, which she recognized from before. "And unless ye plan on gracing Constantine's bed as his mistress, ye'll not want to remain behind when we leave."

"And what if I do?"

He didn't answer her, though his shoulders stiffened when he turned around and ordered his men to ready the ship to pull into port.

"I dinna want to be on your ship another moment." She was close to tears, her chin wobbling, and she clutched her cloak tighter around her, wishing it were more of a fortification.

"This is war, Jane, *war*. Do ye not understand that? Ye dinna get to choose where ye go." He would not look at her, but his words penetrated all the same.

Her mouth fell open a little at that. *War*. She'd not thought of it that way. "Ye intend to get Alexander back?"

"Aye." He left it at that, but it didn't answer any of the questions she had. Why would he choose to go and get him? That would be the honorable thing to do. And he was a pirate, without honor.

A flicker of doubt filled her. Maybe he wasn't as ignoble as she'd thought. But his next words ceased her from thinking anything positive about him.

"Ye think I'm going to let the French have the greatest treasure of Scotland? Bah! It is mine, and I will get it back."

It, as though Alexander were not a person at all.

So it was about vengeance, about getting back the prize he'd lost. The treasure. When it came down to it, that was all he cared about. The coin he would get from returning Alexander to…to who? Livingstone would—

Dear God! Livingstone! The man would pay handsomely

to have Alexander. Not to keep him safe. Nay, to kill him. Had that been Shaw's plan all along?

She couldn't allow that to happen, which meant, she would have to take matters into her own hands. The crossbow came to mind, but the vision of shooting Shaw in his black heart didn't bring her the joy she thought it would. Instead, it brought her grief.

There was no hope for it. Even if she did shoot him, his men would be on her in a second. There would be no mutiny in her honor, they all loved Shaw. Worshipped him.

"I hate ye." Though she spoke the words, they were words only. In her heart, she still loved him deeply, and that made her all the angrier. How could she love someone who had treated her so cruelly? Betrayed her?

His stance tightened. The set of his shoulders made her want to weep. Still, he said nothing. He didn't even turn around so she could look in his eyes and show him just how much he'd hurt her. Well, it didn't matter anyway. As black as his heart was, he wouldn't care.

She whirled around and slammed back into the cabin.

~

An hour or so later, the sun had risen and the ships sailed into the English pirate cove. Thor, Kelly and Lachlan waited on the sandy beach, arms crossed over their chests as though they'd guarded the shore since Shaw had been away the week before.

The men were exhausted and looking forward to a few hours respite, though they were all on alert after the attack at sea. So far, there had been no other sightings of the French or the Spanish, or Livingstone for that matter, but that didn't mean they wouldn't be sailing on the horizon at any minute.

After ordering the crew to dock the ship and settle the

sails, he had Jack assign watch to the men, who'd take shifts between resting, repairing the damage to the ship and guarding against their enemies imminent arrival.

Shaw knocked on the cabin door, hesitant to speak with the woman who deemed him a devil.

"Go away!" she shouted from beyond the wood, and it was not wholly unexpected. In fact, he'd been waiting for it.

He could shoulder his way through the door, demand she speak to him, but somehow, he did not imagine that would go over very well.

"We have docked at Perran." He kept his tone calm, hoping it would soothe her ire.

"Why should I give a fig?" *Ouch*. There was only a bitter bite in her reply.

Shaw kept his temper in check, though he felt his irritation riling. "So ye must open the door and debark the ship."

"I will not."

Shaw gritted his teeth. "Ye've no choice, Jane. Open the door."

"Allow me?" Jane's uncle spoke softly from the bottom of the stairs, his eyes filled with pity that only grated on Shaw's nerves. "'Haps I can reason with her."

Shaw shrugged. "Suit yourself. But if ye canna get her off this ship, ye'll remain here with her."

Edward nodded. "Aye, Captain."

It was the first time Shaw had heard the man call him captain, and he was a little taken aback by it. Well, he didn't have time to dwell on it.

Shaw grunted and trod down the stairs, his limbs heavy.

On the beach, his men greeted him with solemn faces, having heard the news from the crew who'd already debarked.

"Best take care of that," Thor said, nodding toward Shaw's

arm. He'd forgotten the wound he'd sustained on the ship, and blood still seeped from the slice.

The sight of it still didn't sting as much as the rejection from the woman he...*loved*.

"There are more important things to worry over than a trivial wound." Shaw gave his men a grave look. "We were attacked by the Water Bearers at sea. They took the Black Knight and Alexander."

"Damn," Thor growled, his eyes piercing the ocean beyond as though he could call upon the gods to view just where their enemy lay. "We should have been with ye."

Shaw shook his head. "If ye'd come with me, we never would have gotten the two of them out of England. As it was, they were reluctant to join us, and right before they arrived, Santiago, the bastard, came aboard trying to cause trouble."

"So the Spanish and the French are on our tails," Kelly said.

Thor growled, letting out a low curse in regards to Santiago Fernandez, his mortal enemy. Thor had never told him all that happened when he was captured by Santiago some years ago, but they all knew it was horrendous, and ever since then, their brother had wanted to murder the bastard.

"Aye. We'll deal with finding the French first, since they have our treasure, and since I promised Constantine in exchange for our letters of marque, we'd help him gain the French port. And then, Thor, we'll go after the Spanish."

"What of the lass?" Lachlan asked, eyes going toward the ship.

Shaw turned around, trying to hide the hope glittering in his eyes at possibly seeing her coming off the ship. She'd come out of the cabin but did not appear to be debarking. In fact, she looked to be arguing with her uncle. Hands flying, hair wild. Oh, the lass was furious, and he was at a loss as to how to calm her.

"If she knows what's good for her, she'll not be causing me any trouble," Shaw muttered. "And she'll get her arse off my ship."

The men let out low whistles.

Shaw jerked back toward them. "What are ye making that noise for?"

"Ye've fallen for her." Kelly shook his head, made a clucking noise with his tongue.

"I have not," he lied.

"Aye, ye have," Thor added. "Else ye wouldna be so irritated."

"That makes no sense."

"Aye, and she's rebuffed ye," Lachlan remarked.

"To hell with the lot of ye."

He couldn't help turning back around to see that Edward had been able to convince her to get off the ship. She marched down the gangway ahead of him, and on the dock, Jack waited, just as Shaw had asked him to. No doubt, the pirate was overjoyed the lass had finally decided to debark as now he would be able to join the rest of the crew in a bit of respite before they returned to the ship. With war ahead of them, there was little time for rest on the sea, and the crew was likely counting down the minutes they could sleep before their captain steered them back out on to the waters again.

Changing the subject away from the woman, and needing to put distance between them so he wouldn't have to greet her on the beach in front of his men—and possibly, nay definitely, be rebuffed again, he said, "We need to devise a plan of attack." Shaw led his men into the castle where Constantine was already gathering his men around a great oak-planked table. He'd rolled out a map and stabbed a dagger through the place labeled Trésor Cove.

"We sail tonight," Constantine said.

"All my men will travel with us," Shaw agreed.

"And the woman?"

Shaw bristled. "Let me worry about her."

As if on cue, Jane entered the castle, her eyes flashing over Shaw, a blush of fury on her face before she looked away again. She spared no one else a glance, which pleased him more than he wanted to admit.

"She's angry with ye," Constantine pointed out with a chuckle, his blue eyes gleaming with mischief. "'Haps taking her off your hands will be easier said than done."

"Bugger off, ye bastard," Shaw said. "The woman is mine, and I'll see ye sliced end from end before I let ye touch her."

That only made his ally laugh harder. Without thinking, Shaw twisted back around, cocked his fist and slugged Constantine in the jaw. The man stumbled back from the table, confused, but he quickly gathered his wits in a charge that slammed into Shaw's gut. Their men leapt back, ready for what was coming and getting the hell out of the way.

Shaw and Constantine fell to the ground, a fury of flying fists and cursing tongues.

The men around them shouted their excitement at their captains throwing punches as though it were their sworn duty. Had there ever been an occasion they'd spent together that hadn't ended in a brawl?

They'd met by the blade, and they'd likely die by the blade, even if they had periods of friendship in between.

"Stop it!" The shrill demand came from Jane, cutting through the blood that rushed through Shaw's ears and the intense need to pummel Constantine into the stone floor.

Shaw scrambled to his feet, swiping blood from a split lip,

equally pleased to have done as much damage to Constantine. He backed away, resting his hands on his hips.

Constantine, too, climbed to his feet. They were both out of breath, redness on their faces that would likely turn to bruising come morning.

"Apologies, my lady," Shaw said, clearing his throat. "Ye were not meant to bear witness."

"If that was the case, ye wouldna have done it right in front of me." The lady was bristling for a fight, her hands fisted at her sides. He'd never seen her so enraged. If she were in her right mind, she wouldn't have picked her fight with a pirate standing before his entire brethren.

Shaw took measured steps toward her, Constantine and every other man in his way stepping back as they took in the fiery look in his eyes. Jane, however, did not back down. She raised her chin, staring hard at him.

When he was barely a foot from her, Shaw stopped, crowding her space and gazed down at her. The desire to haul her up against him and kiss away that anger was strong. Instead, he took her by the elbow and half dragged her away from her uncle and the prying ears of those who watched them intently. Though out of earshot, they were not completely out of view, and that suited him just fine as it would keep him from kissing her.

"I'm a pirate, wife. Ye knew that when ye met me. When ye wrote to me. When ye begged for my help." Then lower, he said, "Ye knew it when ye gave yourself to me. Dinna insult us both by pretending otherwise."

The tip of her pink tongue darted out to lick her lower lip. She looked ready to say something more, but he stopped her in a hushed tone. "Dinna say another word, lass, or I'll be forced to punish ye. I know ye're angry with me. I know ye want to gouge my eyes out, but look around ye. Remember where ye are. Who they are, who I am. I'm their prince, their leader, and if they see ye disrespecting me, they'll want to see ye get the lash." He didn't dare mention that le Brecque wanted her in his bed—not after what she'd said on the ship.

Redness came to her cheeks, and she bristled. "Ye wouldna."

"If ye forced my hand, I'd take ye over my knee right here and now and give your arse a good spanking."

Her mouth fell open in outrage, fisted hands rising as though she'd pummel him.

Shaw grabbed hold of her fists, bent to kiss them, not allowing her to pull away even as she tugged. "When we're back at Scarba, ye can rail at me all ye like in the privacy of our own chamber, but out here, out in the wilds with pirates drooling for a fight, ye'll keep quiet, else ye see us both killed."

She glanced at the men over his shoulder, perhaps realizing for the first time exactly what kind of position they were in.

"Now curtsy."

"Nay."

"Do it, love, else they think ye continue to disrespect me."

With gritted teeth, she ducked into an indelicate curtsy, and he knew it, but he didn't mind. All he cared about was that she listened, and that it would calm his brethren. When she stood, he bent forward, brushing his lips over hers before she could back away. "'Tis for our safety, lass. Dinna fash yourself, I'll not be coming back to your bed." *Yet.*

Anger radiated from her trembling limbs, but she remained quiet.

"Go and sit by the hearth. We will leave this place soon, but sit where I can see ye and keep ye safe."

She nodded dutifully and did as he asked. And he hated it.

CHAPTER SEVENTEEN

he man is clearly in love with ye.

Uncle Edward's words kept repeating in Jane's mind as she sat on a chair before the hearth in the great hall of Perran Castle. The velvet cushioned perch would have been comfortable if she could actually sit still. In fact, she might have been able to appreciate the castle itself more, if she could focus.

Until Shaw had explained the danger of her situation, and she looked around the great hall at the men filling the space, she hadn't realized how much danger she was in. Glory to him for having made her feel safe. But worse, she felt foolish for not having noticed.

The hall was filled with dozens and dozens of pirate warriors. Maybe even one hundred of them, and only half were Shaw's men. The rest belonged to the man who looked to have been borne of Odin himself.

Every man in the place had more than one weapon strapped to his body. Axes, swords, long hooking or jagged daggers. One man even had a sword that looked like the mouth of a shark with hundreds of rows of jagged teeth. The men were covered in scars, and their eyes glittered with ruthlessness.

A few wenches walked about the great hall, their breasts spilling from their gowns, and a few with a side of their skirts cinched up around their waist to show off not just a part of a leg, but the entire thigh. It was scandalous, as though she'd walked into a den of depravity, and the only moral man among them was her husband—who had just loudly and publicly rebuked her, *after* having loudly and publicly denied her.

Och, what she wouldn't do for a glass of wine, or perhaps even a sip of that hellfire the men were always drinking. Something, anything to calm her nerves. When a wench passed her, Jane caught her attention and begged a cup of wine. But the wench didn't return, and Jane's nerves had yet to abate.

The man is clearly in love with ye.

If Shaw were any other man, she would have laughed in her uncle's face. But he wasn't any other man. He was Savage, prince of the Devils of the Deep. Raised by a pirate king, ruler of his four ships and heir to the brethren, revered by men, feared by many. And loved by her.

If her uncle were to be believed, and why should he even say such unless he believed it, then she needed to truly explore the notion.

The way Shaw loved her was different than what she'd witnessed at court as a young countess—and certainly absent from her own previous marriage, if a child marriage could be called such. And if she thought back far enough, the fact that Shaw had placated her with writing her back over the years meant something. The fact that instead of turning her over his knee to prove a point to his men, he bid her to please be quiet meant something, too.

The man is clearly in love with ye.

Aye, there was an inkling of hope that he might just be. She'd thought so before, too. And though his words had crushed her, maybe they'd been necessary. Because if he'd not denied her, would not that vile devil who'd attacked them tried to do her more harm?

She'd never know. And while her mind screamed to never trust a pirate, her heart adamantly denied that statement. In fact, Shaw was likely the only man she *could* trust.

Around the great table, the men discussed battle strategies. The serving wench finally handed her a mug of ale instead of wine.

"Drink up, love," she said. "You look like you're wasting away."

"Thank ye." Jane took the offered cup from the buxom woman, realizing how waifish she looked beside her. Not caring that it wasn't the wine she asked for, she downed the contents.

Was a buxom woman what Shaw preferred? She recalled that at Scarba the women were rather endowed as well. Her breasts, which she'd never found fault with before, looked rather like unripe apples compared to the overripe gourds on the serving wench's body.

But when she glanced back toward the table, Shaw's gaze was on her, not on the wench, and the way he was looking at her was the way he'd gazed at her in the cabin and on the beach. It was a darkened look full of desire and need and want and possession.

She blushed, realizing that no matter the size of her breasts, he was still looking at her as though she were the most desirous creature in the room.

Perhaps it was time to start seeing him for the man she knew him to be, and to understand the façade he had to keep up as the heir to a pirate kingdom. The only other choice was to make good on her word and leave him once this business

was done, and the thought of no longer having him in her life
left her feeling bereft.

~

THE SUN HAD ALREADY SET WHEN THEY'D LOADED THEIR SHIPS
with supplies and enough cannons to blow an entire country
to bits. Eight ships sailed with the wind at their backs,
pushing them through the blackened waters as though the
sea gods were on their side. When a roll of thunder sounded
overhead, Shaw cursed their fate that a storm would inter-
vene with their mission, but the skies never opened up, only
threatened to for an hour.

"Sky storm," he murmured. Often when they were out at
sea, the gods in the skies liked to taunt them with such, to
keep them alert and at the ready.

"At this speed, we'll reach Trésor Cove by dawn." Jack
took hold of the helm so Shaw could look through his
extended spyglass.

They'd kept well away from the English coast, so as not to
be spotted by the Royal Navy. Eight pirate ships sailing at
high speeds would alert them to an attack, and the last thing
he needed to deal with was the damned English and their
Royal Navy.

Nay, what he was searching for was Livingstone. They'd
yet to run into the man again, but he knew the day was
coming. Livingstone would not have given up so easily. But
the sea surrounding them was clear, not a single light by
which to spot a running ship.

He found his gaze wandering back to the closed cabin
door, beyond which, his wife slept. He wanted to go up there
and knock, or just peek inside to watch her sleep, but he kept
himself below, manning the helm, keeping them on target.
Though he had caught a few hours sleep while Jack took the

helm. He didn't want to be completely exhausted when they finally caught up with Van Rompay and the rest of his demon crew.

By dawn, the coast of Calais was in view, and Shaw turned the helm north toward the caves that made up the pirate town of Trésor Cove. He ordered all lights dimmed, and all eight ships were soon blanketed in darkness. They trimmed back their sails, cutting through the water at a slower pace so that they would wake the French pirates with their cannons and not the sounds or sight of their approach.

And then, there it was. Trésor Cove. The French pirate port that the authorities ignored except when they had enough firepower to completely overtake them—which was rare. The Water Bearers were a ruthless lot and had worked out some sort of arrangement with their government to leave them in peace. In exchange, the Water Bearers would only attack ships not of French nationality. Though that was the arrangement that was made, Shaw believed it might be that Van Rompay's crew were too brutal, too many, to fight against. They didn't fight fair, not by half.

The lights burned from the mouths of the cave, and he imagined the sounds of music and laughter, though they couldn't actually hear it from this distance. Besides, most of the violent, yet oddly cozy-looking town would be asleep at this late hour. Most. He waited, listening for the horn of those men on watch who would spot the moving shadows on the sea, but none came.

"Ready the cannons," Shaw ordered, praying Jane stayed locked up tight in their cabin. "We wake them with a bang. Aim for their ships first." Knowing that Lorne and Alexander would not be aboard the galleys but tucked deep in Van Rompay's dungeon, they would take out their mode of escape first.

They navigated the *Savage of the Sea*, the other ships

following through the water, cutting her at the last moment to point her cannons toward the French ships that lined the cove. Shaw glanced toward Constantine and *The Gaia* to see that he too had pointed his guns toward the shore, and then they gave each other the signal.

"Fire!" Both ships' guns exploded with a bright orange light, the boom a welcome music to Shaw's ears.

The ships in the coves exploded in a violent spray of wood, men screamed in the distance, and warning bells clanged. Kelly, Thor and Lachlan ordered their men to drop into their skiffs and row ashore. Constantine ordered his other captains to do the same, leaving their ships to be manned by their quartermasters. And then they fired again, obliterating all the ships in the cove to smoldering piles of floating wood.

Their men rowed with the force of demons, their white smiles gleaming in the pre-dawn light. Their oars barely made a splash as they propelled themselves with inhuman speed toward shore, battle-lust raging in their blood.

Shaw grinned. "Fire!"

Again, they shot toward the now blazing piles of once great galleys that lit up the cove. There would be nothing left. Shaw wanted to take the French down where it hurt—their ships, their means of enterprise. What was a pirate without a ship? Merely a worthless thug.

Once on shore, if Shaw came across the man who'd dared to touch his wife, he would take great pleasure in gutting the man.

"Ready, Cap'n?" Jack urged him toward the rail where his skiff waited below in the dark water to take him to shore.

"Edward?" Shaw turned around to see that Jane's uncle was ready, a smile on his face and weapons in his hands.

"Aye. Ready as I'll ever be."

"A moment." Shaw broke away from the men, striding

toward the stairs and taking them two at a time. He was about to wrench open the door, if only to see Jane's sweet face one last time before he leapt into the battle, but it swung open when he raised his hand to knock, and she threw herself into his arms.

"Dinna die, Savage," she murmured. "We have a wide ocean to conquer together."

Her words filled him with a swell of turbulent emotions, as deep and dangerous as the ocean below them.

"I'll return," he said.

"Swear to me."

He shouldn't, for to do so was to invite Fate to give him the opposite. So he didn't. Instead, he brushed his lips over hers. And then, because he couldn't help but kiss her more deeply, something he'd not been able to do since the night they'd made love, he wrapped his arms around her and kissed her with all the emotion he felt coiling inside him.

Jane didn't push him away as he feared she might. She pressed herself hard to him and wouldn't let go. In the end, it was him that had to pull free, else he'd pick her up and carry her to bed and forget the battle that sieged outside.

"I love ye." He hadn't meant to say it. The words slipped out without him thinking. A visceral reaction to gazing into her eyes, just as natural to express as it was to breathe or blink.

"I love ye, too, my pirate prince."

They shared one more swift kiss, and then he was sailing down the stairs, leaping over the side of the ship and landing in the skiff below. The battle was in full force by the time he reached the shore.

Shaw yanked his swords from his scabbards, coming at his enemies with a blade in both hand. No mercy. He hacked away at the French on the shore, gaining ground as the minutes ticked by. His men were doing the same.

"No quarter!" Shaw roared.

Constantine echoed his bellows as they made their way closer to the coves and the castle that Van Rompay had built into the side of the mountain.

Shaw knew where the dungeon was. He'd been held there before when he was a lad—taken from MacAlpin's ship during battle. Kept in the deep dark with rats and other vicious things biting at his toes in the night. MacAlpin had found him, saved him, and Shaw had hated the French ever since.

Aye, he'd wanted to lay waste to their coves since he was a lad, and bargaining with Constantine to do just that had been more than a blessing in disguise.

The ships had stopped firing their cannons, but he heard the unmistakable sound of cannon wheels rolling on stone. Inside the castle, Van Rompay must be wheeling cannons to the windows to take aim at the ships beyond. There was no way Van Rompay could fire that far, though he might get close. Shaw bellowed for Jack and the other boatswains left on board to prepare, praying they heard his warning.

Shaw ran toward the cove castle. He had to take out whoever was about to fire the cannons, but Thor stopped him. "I've got the guns, Savage. Go and get the prisoners."

Grunting his thanks, he hacked his way toward the castle and then took a sharp left into the cove, dipping behind a false wall that was wet from where the tide had fallen. The water lapped at his feet, dark and foreboding. He dove inside, spying two guards who gaped at him with surprise in the dim torchlight.

He bared his teeth and swung, taking out the guards, and then he stared at the water where their bodies had just disappeared into the depths. If he didn't remember exactly where the dungeon was, he risked getting lost and drowning, for the dungeon was located in the water, underneath a great stone barrier and then up into a small waterless cavern.

With a prayer to the devil, he slipped into the chilly water and dove deep.

By the time he found the cavern, his lungs were afire. It was not lit in the opening, and he could hear nothing beyond his own gasping breaths.

"Lorne? Alexander?" Shaw called out.

"MacDougall, is that ye?" The Black Knight's voice rang out strong, echoing off the stone.

"Aye. Come toward the sound of my voice. We've not much time."

"The lad is weak."

"If he wants to live, he'll find the will," Shaw said. "Come here, lad. Take my hand."

A hand that was oddly the size of a man's but had the softness of a lad, slipped into his.

"I'm..." The lad's teeth chattered. "'Haps it is best to leave me here."

"Not if I dinna want my wife to kill me," Shaw growled. "Buck up, lad. Ye're borne of kings."

Alexander sucked in a breath, and Shaw dragged him into the water. By the time they got out on the other side, the wee king was coughing up half the sea, as though he'd not even bothered to hold his breath.

Shaw lifted Alexander, flung him over his shoulder and started to run, sword in his free hand and Lorne fighting off French pirates behind him.

They made it over the beach to the skiffs, Scottish pirates blocking the path of the French as Shaw tossed Alexander into the small boat. "Take him back to the ship," Savage said to Lorne.

Edward killed off the man he was fighting and joined them in the lapping waves. Blood soaked the front of his shirt, and for a moment, Shaw thought Jane's uncle might be injured, but he looked hale.

"Ye must come with us," Edward said.

Shaw glanced at the ships in the night, cannon fire from the castle had never sounded. "I've got a score to settle."

With that, Shaw left them at the skiff, certain that his men would see the three of them to the ship and that his wife would disobey him and exit her cabin to tend to the lad.

Searching the beach, he made out the retreating figure of Van Rompay slipping up the stone stairs carved into the side of the cliffs.

"Ye're not getting away from me this time, ye bastard," Shaw growled.

He took off at a run, blocking a pirate who swung his sword, and leaping over another that tried to drag him down to the ground. No one was going to get in the way of him exacting vengeance on Van Rompay.

And then Constantine joined him, mouth hard in a firm line and eyes blazing with power and rage. Blood splattered across his face, covered the bruises from their earlier skirmish. "Let me, Savage. He's mine. Trésor Cove is mine. We made a deal."

Shaw let out a frustrated growl. He wanted to be the one to end that bastard's life, but knowing that Constantine had a greater debt that needed to be paid, he would oblige his friend. "Bring me his head."

"Aye, you'll have it." And then his greatest ally was slipping up the stairs silently behind the man who'd been behind so much torment in both of their lives.

It was over. Time to return to Scarba and begin anew.

Time to realize that the woman he couldn't live without didn't make him more vulnerable. If anything, he felt stronger.

CHAPTER EIGHTEEN

"*H*and me that bandage," Jane ordered Lorne.

She wrapped it around the now cleaned up wound Alexander had sustained at some point during his captivity.

"A meal for the lad," she ordered Jack, who in turn bellowed the order to a swab.

Since Lorne, Alexander and her Uncle Edward had returned to the ship, she'd seen to it that they were taken care of. Getting each of them cleaned up, fed. As the wife of the captain of this ship, that was her duty, was it not?

She was just about to order a cot be brought to her cabin for the lad to rest on when she spotted Shaw making his way back toward the ship.

In the pink and hazy dawn light, he stood upon a small skiff and rowed himself back toward shore. A tall, dark, devastatingly handsome devil upon the gently lapping waves. Behind him, the French cove had fallen, Scottish and English pirates alike were returning to their ships.

They'd won.

Her heart skipped a beat, and she might have stopped breathing.

This man, this warrior who floated over the water like he owned the ocean, was all hers.

Jane ran to the side of the boat, hands splayed on the wood, taking in the sight of him as though she thought the sea were playing tricks on her. And then a second later, he was there at the bottom of the rope, climbing swiftly as though his own weight were nothing, hand over massive hand, eyes on her the entire time. At the top of the ladder, he gazed at her for half a heartbeat before his lips crashed onto hers. She didn't even feel him climb over the side or lift her up and carry her up the stairs to their cabin—which at the moment she was eternally grateful she'd not gotten around to ordering a cot placed in for Alexander.

Their lips were molten, and the kiss so passionate, she didn't notice Shaw shredding the clothes from both their bodies. She was so intent on his kiss, on the press of his hard body to hers, she hardly felt it until he came crashing down on her, his skin sliding naked over hers. The heated contact of his rigid body, full of steely muscle, pressed to her softer self, the tickle of his hair on her bare skin. Heaven help her...

"Oh, Jane, my love," he murmured against her ear, sending frissons of passion and need sweeping through her from head to toe. "When I thought of ye leaving me..."

"I would never leave ye." She pressed heated kisses over his face, tugging him closer, wishing to melt inside him. "Even when I said it, I couldna do it. Ye're a part of me. Ye have been for years. There is nothing that could make me go."

"I'm sorry, love. I'm so sorry for the things I said. I'm so sorry they captured ye. Touched ye. I'm so sorry," he murmured against her skin.

"Ye only said those things to keep me safe. Ye didna order

them to take me from our cabin." She clutched his shoulders, scraping her taut nipples against the expanse of his chest and shuddering. She wrapped her legs high around his hips, needing him to take possession of her. "I'm safe. I've always been safe, because of ye."

"I never want ye to be used like that. To be a pawn. That is not what I want for ye." His lips trailed over her chest, taking the nipple she offered into his mouth and sucking deep.

"I know, Shaw, I know."

"God, I love the way ye taste." And he moved lower, nipping at her hip as he pressed her thighs wide with his hands and gazed at the very heated, hot center of her. "I want to taste all of ye."

Jane allowed him to slide his tongue along the seam of her mons, to tease her for a few moments, but what she really wanted was for him to be inside her. To look into his eyes as he thrust deep, and tell him over and over again how much she loved him, needed him.

"Shaw, please," she begged. "I want ye inside me."

He growled against her hot core and lifted up, hooking her legs around his hips and placing himself at her center. Gazing into her eyes, he plunged hard, filling her. Owning her.

"God, I love ye," he said.

Jane's heart melted then, the words falling from her lips in a torrent as pleasure crashed over her.

Shaw's thrusts were wild, and she lifted her hips to meet each frantic plunge, desperate for him. Incredible sensations radiated limb from limb, and the intensity of it coiled inside her. But with it all, as he stared down at her, pure love in his eyes, she knew she'd found her one and only, her true love.

≈

LYING IN BED TWO DAYS LATER, JANE CURLED ON HER SIDE around Shaw, drew circles on his chest.

He coiled her hair around his fingers. "We'll be arriving in Scarba soon."

"I want to meet the mysterious King MacAlpin."

Shaw chuckled. "He's terrifying."

"He canna be as terrifying as ye, Savage." She placed a kiss over his heart.

"Where do ye think I learned to be this ruthless?" Shaw stiffened. "Dammit," he cursed under his breath, sitting up, and then swiftly leaving the warmth of their bed.

"What is it?"

"I dinna know. But the men are disturbed by something."

How could he even tell? He'd mentioned that since they'd returned from Trésor Cove, his senses had been heightened, and that he believed that allowing himself to love her had actually set him free of the prison he'd been keeping himself locked up in. Whatever that meant. She was just happy he was happy, and she'd never experienced such bliss in all her days.

Shaw quickly drew on his breeches and top, not bothering to tie the laces as he charged from the room, turning around swiftly to grab his sword as he went.

Jane quickly dressed, just in case they were about to be boarded and another heinous pirate thought it a good idea to take her in hand. She shuddered at the thought of the last bastard to have done so. Then snickered at her use of *bastard*. She really was becoming like her husband.

She wrapped a gold-braided belt around the soft, practical, green wool gown. As it turned out, the sea spray wasn't what ended up ruining her beautiful blue silk one, but Shaw's primal need upon returning from battle when he'd fairly ripped it from her body.

Before she'd put on her shoes, the ship jolted with the force of their own cannons firing.

"Nay!" Not again! They were *so* close to home.

Home.

Though she'd only been to the castle on Scarba once, she would make it her home. Any place that Shaw was would be her place.

And no way in hell was she going to let anyone attack her home.

Jane marched to the cabinet full of weapons and yanked open the doors. The crossbow was hanging in the exact same spot it had been in before. She grabbed it along with the quiver and a dagger that she tucked into the braided belt at her waist.

If she was truly going to embrace being a pirate's wife, the mistress of Castle Dheomhan, she had better start by defending her prince's ship.

Jane opened the door, the crossbow hanging at her side, and was momentarily stunned.

They were not just being attacked by anyone—it was their greatest enemy. Livingstone.

She'd not seen him for five long years, and she could have lived happily never seeing him again. He stood at the bow of his ship, staring right at her, an evil grin on his face as though he were saying, *I've got ye.*

Shaw, catching sight of her, bellowed, "Get back inside."

Livingstone might have opened fire, but the Devils of the Deep were quick to return the fire. This time, Livingstone had brought reinforcements. There were three of his ships compared to Shaw's four, which weren't good odds for the royal vassal, but it appeared the man had drawn a line in the sand and was bringing this fight to full closure.

"Bloody fool," she murmured.

The other ships belonging to the Devils of the Deep moved in on the two ships flanking Livingstone.

Jane could barely hear herself think, let alone the repeated bellows from her husband. All around her, men cried out as death met them at the end of a blade or they were torn apart by cannon fire, speared by flying pieces of splintered wood. This was the French cove all over again, except victory wasn't so easily predicted.

"For the love of God, get back inside," Shaw shouted at her again.

Stunned, Jane glanced down at the crossbow in her hand and realized how foolish she'd been to think she'd be able to help. Already she was distracting Shaw enough that he didn't have his full attention on the battle. So she did as he asked and backed into the cabin, shutting the door behind her, pressing her hand to the wood and breathing deeply. That was the best way she could help him—not to be in his way.

There were a lot of things Jane could do. She could tend the sick, mend clothes, run a household and please her husband. But she was no help in battle. She'd only be in the way.

"Nay." She stared at the splintered bar that had yet to be replaced because they'd been so busy in their love nest.

There was no way to block a man out as all the furniture in the room was nailed to the floor. Well, if anyone were to break into the cabin, she would blow them away with the crossbow. No one was going to take her like they'd done before.

She just prayed the next man to walk through the door was her husband.

Jane wasn't certain how much time had passed between sitting on the chair to stare at the door, and when the cannon fire finally ebbed. But it was long enough that she was trembling and fairly certain Shaw was dead and she would soon be Livingstone's victim again.

So when the door handle lifted, she cocked the crossbow, lifted it and closed her eyes.

"Open your damn eyes and put that thing down afore ye shoot me!" Shaw's voice was a welcome relief.

Her eyes snapped open, and she almost dropped the crossbow in her haste to run to him, but instead she hurried to unhook the latch and then bolted into his warm embrace. She didn't care that he was covered in dusty ash and blood. She just wanted to feel his arms around her.

"Come. I've a present for ye." His voice was gruff, gravelly from yelling.

"A present?" She shook her head, confused. "Shaw, we're in the middle of a battle."

He shook his head. "It is done. Now come collect your gift."

"Done? Livingstone?" She bit her lip, not daring to hope that they wouldn't be bothered by him every again.

"Come, and ye shall see."

"All right." She hooked her arm around his and followed him out of the cabin, fearful that she'd see their enemy skinned and hanging from the gibbet.

Well, he had all of his skin, and he wasn't hanging from the gibbet, but Livingstone was sputtering mad and tied to the mast. Several of his men were kneeling on the ground around him.

Shaw hadn't called *no quarter.* To say she was surprised was an understatement. She expected to come out of the cabin to see complete and utter carnage.

"I thought ye'd like to witness me dispatching the man who shattered your life."

Oh... He'd brought her out to observe the execution. She swallowed hard around the lump in her throat. It was one thing to find out after the fact that their enemy had been vanquished in battle, but to attend the execution of a defenseless man tied to a mast… It left a sick feeling in the pit of her stomach. She knew this was the pirate life. That she should accept it. But perhaps just this once, as he'd claimed Livingstone was her gift, she could beg a pardon.

"Do ye have to kill him?" Jane implored Shaw with her eyes, though she'd said it softly enough not to let anyone else know just what she'd said. No use having her husband angry at her for trying to go against him in front of his brethren. "If not for him, I would never have met ye."

Shaw grunted. "Dead men tell no tales, love." The struggle in his visage was real. He wanted to give her what she wanted, but he had a duty to see his people safe, and a repu-tation to uphold. "But perhaps, we can leave his death up to Fate, given he did bring us together."

At that, she quirked a brow and saw that his gaze had gone out toward the open sea. This was the perhaps the most mercy that Livingstone could ever hope to receive. "Aye, up to Fate."

Shaw glared at Livingstone, and for a moment, judging from the anger on Shaw's face, Jane was pretty certain that her gentle warrior had changed his mind. But then his lip twitched in a cruel smile. He pulled out his sword, and Jane stiffened. He had changed his mind.

When he brought the sword down on Livingstone, Jane closed her eyes, unable to watch. But then she heard his next words, and they had her peeking through them again. He'd not hacked the man down, but instead cut through the ropes that had tied him to the mast.

"Jump," Shaw said. "If the fates be kind to ye, ye'll float all the way back to the mainland."

Livingstone swallowed hard, perhaps deciding whether it would be better to just accept death as his fortune, but then he nodded and leapt into the water with a great splash. They watched as he proceeded to swim like a maniac toward shore.

"Slow down, else ye tire too quickly and drown," Shaw warned.

Jane tucked her arm around her husband's, giving him a squeeze and smiling. "I'm impressed, husband. Ye didna have to warn him of the risks of exhaustion."

"Nay, but then I'd not be living up to my promise to ye to give him a chance."

She smiled and curled into him. "How could I have ever thought ye werena honorable?"

Shaw chuckled and pointed at the carnage of Livingstone's ship. "I have no idea, we've only destroyed a king's ship and sent a government official to swim with the sharks."

"Where are the rest of them?" But as she asked, she searched out the horizon and saw that the royal vessels had abandoned Livingstone to his fate. "Now what?"

"Perhaps now I shall present to my father, King MacAlpin, his new pirate prince."

"New?" Jane frowned. "What do ye mean?"

"Aye, new. Did ye not see the way Alexander's eyes glittered during the battle? Forget ruling Scotland, he's got the blood of a pirate in him."

Jane laughed, gazing out over the ship to see that Alexander was pestering Jack with a million questions at once.

"Aye, husband, I think ye're right. But where will that leave ye?"

"We've got many years yet before he would take my place. Until then, I plan to sweep my wife off her feet and give her every jewel her heart might desire."

Jane clucked her tongue. "Only if it is paid for."

Shaw chuckled. "Aye. Paid in full."

"And not with blood."

He bent to kiss her then. "Ye do recall I'm a pirate, nay?"

"A most noble and honorable pirate."

"Only when it comes to ye, my love. Only ye." With that, he shouted orders for the men to make haste to the dock, and then whispered in her ear, "For I've a lady to conquer."

EPILOGUE

One year and one month later

*T*he great hall smelled like a damned garden.

Shaw scowled. Why had he brought his wife all those sweet-smelling dried herbs and flowers, and the scented oils from the Barbary ship he'd sacked?

"Where is everyone?" he called out.

The great hall was empty, not the usual den of debauchery. The hearth was in full blaze, but no one was tending it.

"Oh, there ye are." Jane came flouncing from behind a screen at the back of the great hall that hadn't been there before.

"What's happened?"

"Oh." She grinned, glancing around herself with pride. "I just made it a little more…hospitable."

What was he missing? "I thought it was plenty hospitable before."

"Oh, 'haps for a bachelor pirate, but not for his wife. Trust me, the last thing I want to see as I grow fatter are the brazen lassies flaunting their wares."

"As ye grow fatter?" That didn't make sense. He'd not been gone long, a few months perhaps. But he'd made sure to return just now, as it was November, and the anniversary of the day they'd met.

Jane pressed her hands to her belly, and he noticed then the swell beneath her gown. How the hell could he have missed it? She *was* fatter.

"Plus, I didna think it right for our child to be born into a den of iniquity."

A child? She was holding her belly. There was the rounded swell... Why did he feel like he'd suddenly lost the capacity to think clearly? Did that mean...? "Ye're with child?"

Jane beamed up at him. "I am. 'Tis yours, in case ye were wondering." She winked at him in that teasing way she had. "Constantine did stop by to see about another arrangement with ye, but I assure ye I didna let him in my bed. Though I was tempted after ye left me for so long."

Shaw snorted, though inside there was still a slight twinge of jealousy that Constantine had seen her before he had. "Och, lass, do ye want me to go to battle?"

She laughed all the harder, then went to a sideboard he'd never seen before and poured him a mug of ale. "Here ye go."

"Ye've turned my great hall into a home."

That made her smile widen and her blue eyes sparkle with pleasure. "Our home. Our family's home."

"So, where did ye put everyone? Did ye banish them from the island?"

She laughed, the tinkling sound echoing off the rafters and stones and warming his insides. How he'd missed her. "Oh, nay, silly. I turned the old barracks into a..." She blushed. "Well, I wouldna call it a brothel exactly. I've been calling it the *pirate's point*, simply because when I see a pirate enter the castle, I've been pointing."

"The old barracks, what did ye do with my treasure that was guarded there day and night by my men?"

"Some things I put to use in the house, like this lovely table and that tapestry, and well, this I took for myself." She pointed to a diamond necklace at her throat. "The rest of it I had placed in your new treasury."

Shaw narrowed his eyes. "I liked my old treasury."

Jane put her hands on her hips and glowered up at her husband. "And *I* like not finding an orgy on my breakfast table."

Good God, he'd never heard her say that word before. He hadn't thought she'd even know what it meant. And that made him chuckle. What a different lass she was from the innocent he'd saved six years before. But no matter how exposed she was to the baser ways of life, she always remained sweet and good to him.

"Excellent point, my love." He pulled her in for an embrace, calming some of her ire by kissing the breath from her. "Now, show me the new treasury."

"I thought ye'd want to keep an eye on it, so I had it moved to the north tower taking up the entire level above our rooms."

He twirled a tendril of her hair around his finger. So silky. He leaned forward, breathing her in. Triton's trident, he loved the scent of her—floral and a vague hint of spice, and something else that nudged at his possessive side. "Ah, a good place for it."

"Aye." She giggled. "There was nothing up there, save a few dusty broken chairs and a decade's worth of cobwebs."

"And where will the bairn sleep?"

"In the chamber opposite ours." She wrapped her arms around his middle and gazed up at him. "I know it is not customary for a nursery to be so close to the master chamber, but I dinna think I will be able to bear being so far from our bairn, especially when I must spend so much time away from ye."

"I could not deny ye that, my love." And he kissed her again, and then gazed deep into her eyes. "A bairn. Our bairn."

"Aye, another prince."

"Or a princess."

She grinned. "Aye."

"Speaking of princes, how is Alexander?"

Jane chuckled. "Well, it has been a feat of pure skill to keep him away from pirate's point, I can tell ye that much, but he has been spending a lot of time with Thor while ye were gone. I think he's taken a liking to the man."

Shaw grinned. "Ye really have worked magic. Thor is the least tolerant of anyone under the age of twenty summers."

Jane rolled her eyes. "It helps that Alexander treats him like a god. He may have given him a big head, to be honest."

"Thor with a bigger ego than before? Impossible."

"I assure ye, it is quite a thing to see."

Shaw let out a low rumble of a laugh. "And your father? When will he arrive? He'll not have me arrested for Livingstone, will he? He's not planning to arrive with a dozen ships?"

Jane pressed her hand to his heart, making it jump all the more. "Nay, my love. Never. While he is in disagreement with your chosen profession, he would never harm the man who risked his life for me more than once."

Shaw wrapped her up in his arms, kissing her deeply. "I would do it all over again."

"Speaking of that…" She winked. "There is something else ye should know."

"What is it?" God, he loved the sparkle in her eyes.

"I've learned how to use the crossbow verra well now. Thor says I'm a natural."

Shaw laughed with pure joy. "I never had any doubt."

EXCERPT FROM THE HIGHLANDER'S GIFT

CHAPTER ONE

Dupplin Castle
Scottish Highlands
Winter, 1318

Sir Niall Oliphant had lost something.

Not a trinket, or a boot. Not a pair of hose, or even his favorite mug. Nothing as trivial as that. In fact, he wished it *was* so minuscule that he could simply replace it. What'd he'd lost was devastating, and yet it felt entirely selfish given some of those closest to him had lost their lives.

He was still here, living and breathing. He was still walking around on his own two feet. Still handsome in the face. Still able to speak coherently, even if he didn't want to.

But he couldn't replace what he'd lost.

What he'd lost would irrevocably change his life, his entire future. It made him want to back into the darkest corner and let his life slip away, to forget about even having a future at all. To give everything he owned to his brother and say goodbye. He was useless now. Unworthy.

Niall cleared the cobwebs that had settled in his throat by slinging back another dram of whisky. The shutters in his darkened bedchamber were closed tight, the fire long ago grown cold. He didn't allow candles in the room, nor visitors. So when a knock sounded at his door, he ignored it, preferring to chug his spirits from the bottle rather than pouring it into a cup.

The knocking grew louder, more insistent.

"Go away," he bellowed, slamming the whisky down on the side table beside where he sat, and hearing the clay jug shatter. A shard slid into his finger, stinging as the liquor splashed over it. But he didn't care.

This pain, pain in his only index finger, he wanted to have. Wanted a reminder there was still some part of him left. Part of him that could still feel and bleed. He tried to ignore that part of him that wanted to be alive, however small it was.

The handle on the door rattled, but Niall had barred it the day before. Refusing anything but whisky. Maybe he could drink himself into an oblivion he'd never wake from. Then all of his worries would be gone forever.

"Niall, open the bloody door."

The sound of his brother's voice through the cracks had Niall's gaze widening slightly. Walter was a year younger than he was. And still whole. Walter had tried to understand Niall's struggle, but what man could who'd not been through it himself?

"I said go away, ye bloody whoreson." His words slurred, and he went to tipple more of the liquor only to recall he'd just shattered it everywhere.

Hell and damnation. The only way to get another bottle would be to open the door.

"I'll pretend I didna hear ye just call our dear mother a whore. Open the damned door, or I'll take an axe to it."

Like hell he would. Walter was the least aggressive one in their family. Sweet as a lad, he'd grown into a strong warrior, but he was also known as the heart of the Oliphant clan. The idea of him chopping down a door was actually funny. Outside, the corridor grew silent, and Niall leaned his head back against the chair, wondering how long he had until his brother returned, and if it was enough time to sneak down to the cellar and get another jug of whisky.

Needless to say, when a steady thwacking sounded at the door—reminding Niall quite a bit like the heavy side of an axe—he sat up straighter and watched in drunken fascination as the door started to splinter. Shards of wood came flying through the air as the hole grew larger and the sound of the axe beating against the surface intensified.

Walter had grown some bloody ballocks.

Incredible.

Didn't matter. What would Walter accomplish by breaking down the door? What could he hope would happen?

Niall wasn't going to leave the room or accept food.

Niall wasn't going to move on with his life.

So he sat back and waited, curious more than anything as to what Walter's plan would be once he'd gained entry.

Just as tall and broad of shoulder as Niall, Walter kicked through the remainder of the door and ducked through the ragged hole.

"That's enough." Walter looked down at Niall, his face fierce, reminding him very much of their father when they were lads.

"That's enough?" Niall asked, trying to keep his eyes wide but having a hard time. The light from the corridor gave his brother a darkened, shadowy look.

"Ye've sat in this bloody hell hole for the past three days." Walter gestured around the room. "Ye stink of shite. Like a bloody pig has laid waste to your chamber."

"Are ye calling me a shite pig?" Niall thought about standing up, calling his brother out, but that seemed like too much effort.

"Mayhap I am. Will it make ye stand up any faster?"

Niall pursed his lips, giving the impression of actually considering it. "Nay."

"That's what I thought. But I dinna care. Get up."

Niall shook his head slowly. "I'd rather not."

"I'm not asking."

My, my. Walter's ballocks were easily ten times than Niall had expected. The man was bloody testing him to be sure.

"Last time I checked, I was the eldest," Niall said.

"Ye might have been born first, but ye lost your mind some time ago, which makes me the better fit for making decisions."

Niall hiccupped. "And what decisions would ye be making, wee brother?"

"Getting your arse up. Getting ye cleaned up. Airing out the gongheap."

"Doesna smell so bad in here." Niall gave an exaggerated sniff, refusing to admit that Walter was indeed correct. It smelled horrendous.

"I'm gagging, brother. I might die if I have to stay much longer."

"Then by all means, pull up a chair."

"Ye're an arse."

"No more so than ye."

"Not true."

Niall sighed heavily. "What do ye want? Why would ye make me leave? I've nothing to live for anymore."

"Ye've eight-thousand reasons to live, ye blind goat."

"Eight thousand?"

"A random number." Walter waved his hand and kicked at something on the floor. "Ye've the people of your clan, the warriors ye lead, your family. The woman ye're betrothed to marry. Everyone is counting on ye, and ye must come out of here and attend to your duties. Ye've mourned long enough."

"How can ye presume to tell me that I've mourned long enough? Ye know nothing." A slow boiling rage started in Niall's chest. All these men telling him how to feel. All these men thinking they knew better. A bunch of bloody ballocks!

"Aye, I've not lost what ye have, brother. Ye're right. I dinna know what 'tis like to be ye, either. But I know what 'tis like to be the one down in the hall waiting for ye to come and take care of your business. I know what 'tis like to look upon the faces of the clan as they worry about whether they'll be raided or ravaged while their leader sulks in a vat of whisky and does nothing to care for them."

Niall gritted his teeth. No one understood. And he didn't need the reminder of his constant failings.

"Then take care of it," Niall growled, jerking forward fast enough that his vision doubled. "Ye've always wanted to be first. Ye've always wanted what was mine. Go and have it. Have it all."

Walter took a step back as though Niall had hit him. "How can ye say that?" Even in the dim light, Niall could see the pain etched on his brother's features. Aye, what he'd said was a lie, but it had made him feel better all the same.

"Ye heard me. Get the fuck out." Niall moved to push himself from the chair, remembered too late how difficult that would be, and fell back into it. Instead, he let out a string of curses that had Walter shaking his head.

"Ye need to get yourself together, decide whether or not ye are going to turn your back on this clan. Do it for yourself. Dinna go down like this. Ye are still Sir Niall fucking

Oliphant. Warrior. Heir to the chiefdom of Oliphant. Hero. Leader. Brother. Soon to be husband and father."

Walter held his gaze unwaveringly. A torrent of emotion jabbed from that dark look into Niall's chest, crushing his heart.

"Get out," he said again through gritted teeth, feeling the pain of rejecting his brother acutely.

They'd always been so close. And even though he was pushing him away, he also desperately wanted to pull him closer.

He wanted to hug him tightly, to tell him not to worry, that soon enough he'd come out of the dark and be the man Walter once knew. But those were all lies, for he would never be the same again, and he couldn't see how he would ever be able to exit this room and attempt a normal life.

"Ye're not the only one who's lost a part of himself," Walter muttered as he ducked beneath the door. "I want my brother back."

"Your brother is dead."

At that, Walter paused. He turned back around, a snarl poised on his lips, and Niall waited longingly for whatever insult would come out. Any chance to engage in a fight, but then Walter's face softened. "Maybe he is."

With those soft words uttered, he disappeared, leaving behind the gaping hole and the shattered wood on the floor, a haunting mirror image to the wide-open wound Niall felt in his soul.

Niall glanced down to his left, at the sleeve that hung empty at his side, a taunting reminder of his failure in battle. Warrior. Ballocks! Not even close.

When he considered lying down on the ground and licking the whisky from the floor, he knew it was probably time to leave his chamber. But he was no good to anyone outside of his room. Perhaps he could prove that fact once and for all, then Walter would leave him be. And he knew his brother spoke the truth about smelling like a pig. He'd not bathed in days. If he was going to prove he was worthless as a leader now, he would do so smelling decent, so people took him seriously rather than believing him to be mad.

Slipping through the hole in the door, he walked noiselessly down the corridor to the stairs at the rear used by the servants, tripping only once along the way. He attempted to steal down the winding steps, a feat that nearly had him breaking his neck. In fact, he took the last dozen steps on his arse. Once he reached the entrance to the side of the bailey, he lifted the bar and shoved the door open, the cool wind a welcome blast against his heated skin. With the sun set, no one saw him creep outside and slink along the stone as he made his way to the stables and the massive water trough kept for the horses. He might as well bathe there, like the animal he was.

Trough in sight, he staggered forward and tumbled head-first into the icy water.

Niall woke sometime later, still in the water, but turned over at least. He didn't know whether to be grateful he'd not drowned. His clothes were soaked, and his legs hung out on either side of the wooden trough. It was still dark, so at least he'd not slept through the night in the chilled water.

He leaned his head back, body covered in wrinkled gooseflesh and teeth chattering, and stared up at the sky. Stars dotted the inky-black landscape and swaths of clouds streaked across the moon, as if one of the gods had swiped his hand through it, trying to wipe it away. But the moon was steadfast. Silver and bright and ever present. Returning as it should each night, though hiding its beauty day after day until it was just a sliver that made one wonder if it would return.

What was he doing out here? Not just in the tub freezing

his idiot arse off, but here in this world? Why hadn't he been taken? Why had only part of him been stolen? Cut away…

Niall shuddered, more from the memory of that moment when his enemy's sword had cut through his armor, skin, muscle and bone. The crunching sound. The incredible pain.

He squeezed his eyes shut, forcing the memories away.

This is how he'd been for the better part of four months. Stumbling drunk and angry about the castle when he wasn't holed up in his chamber. Yelling at his brother, glowering at his father and mother, snapping at anyone who happened to cross his path. He'd become everything he hated.

There had been times he'd thought about ending it all. He always came back to the simple question that was with him now as he stared up at the large face of the moon.

"Why am I still here?" he murmured.

"Likely because ye havena pulled your arse out of the bloody trough."

Walter.

Niall's gaze slid to the side to see his brother standing there, arms crossed over his chest. "Are ye my bloody shadow? Come to tell me all my sins?"

"When will ye see I'm not the enemy? I want to help."

Niall stared back up at the moon, silently asking what he should do, begging for a sign.

Walter tugged at his arm. "Come on. Get out of the trough. Ye're not a pig as much as ye've been acting the part. Let us get ye some food."

Niall looked over at his little brother, perhaps seeing him for the first time. His throat felt tight, closing in on itself as a well of emotion overflowed from somewhere deep in his gut.

"Why do ye keep trying to help me? All I've done is berate ye for it."

"Aye. That's true, but I know ye speak from pain. Not from your heart."

"I dinna think I have a heart left."

Walter rolled his eyes and gave a swift tug, pulling him halfway from the trough. Though Niall was weak from lack of food and too much whisky, he managed to get himself the rest of the way out. He stood in the moonlight, dripping water around the near frozen ground.

"Ye have a heart. Ye have a soul. One arm. That is all ye've lost. Ye still have your manhood, aye?"

Niall shrugged. Aye, he still had his bloody cock, but what woman wanted a decrepit man heaving overtop of her with his mangled body in full view.

"I know what ye're thinking," Walter said. "And the answer is, every eligible maiden and all her friends. Not to mention the kitchen wenches, the widows in the glen, and their sisters."

"Ballocks," Niall muttered.

"Ye're still handsome. Ye're still heir to a powerful clan. Wake up, man. This is not ye. Ye canna let the loss of your arm be the destruction of your whole life. Ye're not the first man to ever be maimed in battle. Dinna be a martyr."

"Says the man with two arms."

"Ye want me to cut it off? I'll bloody do it." Walter turned in a frantic circle as if looking for the closest thing with a sharp edge.

Niall narrowed his eyes, silent, watching, waiting. When had his wee brother become such an intense force? Walter marched toward the barn, hand on the door, yanked it wide as if to continue the blockhead search. Niall couldn't help following after his brother who marched forward with purpose, disappearing inside the barn.

A flutter of worry dinged in Niall's stomach. Walter wouldn't truly go through with something so stupid, would he?

When he didn't immediately reappear, Niall's pang of

worry heightened into dread. Dammit, he just might. With all the changes Walter had made recently, there was every possibility that he'd gone mad. Well, Niall might wish to disappear, but not before he made certain his brother was all right.

With a groan, Niall lurched forward, grabbed the door and yanked it open. The stables were dark and smelled of horses, leather and hay. He could hear a few horses nickering, and the soft snores of the stable hands up on the loft fast asleep.

"Walter," he hissed. "Enough. No more games."

Still, there was silence.

He stepped farther into the barn, and the door closed behind him, blocking out all the light save for a few strips that sank between cracks in the roof.

His feet shuffled silently on the dirt floor. Where the bloody hell had his brother gone?

And why was his heart pounding so fiercely? He trudged toward the first set of stables, touching the wood of the gates. A horse nudged his hand with its soft muzzle, blowing out a soft breath that tickled his palm, and Niall's heart squeezed.

"Prince," he whispered, leaning his forehead down until he felt it connect with the warm, solidness of his warhorse. Prince nickered and blew out another breath.

Niall had not ridden in months. If not for his horse, he might be dead. But rather than be irritated Prince had done his job, he felt nothing but pride that the horse he'd trained from a colt into a mammoth had done his duty.

After Niall's arm had been severed and he was left for dead, Prince had nudged him awake, bent low and nipped at Niall's legs until he'd managed to crawl and heave himself belly first over the saddle. Prince had taken him home like that, a bleeding sack of grain.

Having thought him dead, the clan had been shocked and

surprised to see him return, and that's when the true battle for his life had begun. He'd lost so much blood, succumbed to fever, and stopped breathing more than once. Hell, it was a miracle he was still alive.

Which begged the question—*why, why, why...*

"He's missed ye." Walter was beside him, and Niall jerked toward his brother, seeing his outline in the dark.

"Is that why ye brought me in here?"

"Did ye really think I'd cut off my arm?" Walter chuckled. "Ye know I like to fondle a wench and drink at the same time."

Niall snickered. "Ye're an arse."

"Aye, 'haps I am."

They were silent for a few minutes, Niall deep in thought as he stroked Prince's soft muzzle. His mind was a torment of unanswered questions. "Walter, I...I dinna know what to do."

"Take it one day at a time, brother. But do take it. No more being locked in your chamber."

Niall nodded even though his brother couldn't see him. A phantom twinge of pain rippled through the arm that was no longer there, and he stopped himself from moving to rub the spot, not wanting to humiliate himself in front of his brother. When would those pains go away? When would his body realize his arm had long since become bone in the earth?

One day at a time. That was something he might be able to do. "I'll have bad days."

"Aye. And good ones, too."

Niall nodded. He longed to saddle Prince and go for a ride but realized he wasn't even certain how to mount with only one arm to grab hold of the saddle. "I have so much to learn."

"Aye. But as I recall, ye're a fast learner."

"I'll start training again tomorrow."

"Good."

"But I willna be laird. Walter, the right to rule is yours now."

"Ye've time before ye need to make that choice. Da is yet breathing and making a ruckus."

"Aye. But I want ye to know what's coming. No matter what, I canna do that. I have to learn to pull on my bloody shirt first."

Walter slapped him on the back and squeezed his shoulder. "The lairdship is yours, with or without a shirt. Only thing I want is my brother back."

Niall drew in a long, mournful breath. "I'm not sure he's coming back. Ye'll have to learn to deal with me, the new me."

"New ye, old ye, still *ye*."

Want to read the rest of The Highlander's Gift?

Guarded by the Warrior

The MacDougall Legacy Series:

Laird of Shadows

Laird of Twilight

Laird of Darkness

The Thistles and Roses Series

Promise of a Knight

Eternally Bound

Breath from the Sea

The Highland Bound Series: (Erotic time-travel)

Behind the Plaid

Bared to the Laird

Dark Side of the Laird

Highlander's Touch

Highlander Undone

Highlander Unraveled

Draped in Plaid

Wicked Women:

Her Desperate Gamble

Seducing the Sheriff

Kiss Me, Cowboy

∼

Under the name E. Knight

Tales From the Tudor Court

My Lady Viper

Prisoner of the Queen

Ancient Historical Fiction:

A Day of Fire: a novel of Pompeii

A Year of Ravens: a novel of Boudica's Rebellion

ABOUT THE AUTHOR

Eliza Knight is an award-winning and *USA Today* bestselling indie author of over fifty sizzling historical romance and erotic romance. Under the name E. Knight, she pens rip-your-heart-out historical fiction. While not reading, writing or researching for her latest book, she chases after her three children. In her spare time (if there is such a thing…) she likes daydreaming, wine-tasting, traveling, hiking, staring at the stars, watching movies, shopping and visiting with family and friends. She lives atop a small mountain with her own knight in shining armor, three princesses and two very naughty puppies. Visit Eliza at http://www.elizaknight.com or her historical blog History Undressed: www.historyundressed.com. Sign up for her newsletter to get news about books, events, contests and sneak peaks! http://eepurl.com/CSFFD

facebook.com/elizaknightfiction

twitter.com/elizaknight

instagram.com/elizaknightfiction

bookbub.com/authors/eliza-knight

goodreads.com/elizaknight

pinterest.com/authoreknight

Made in the USA
Middletown, DE
30 April 2021